D0200409

Date Due

JUN 1 4 '76			
JUL 8 '76			
JUN 9 78			
AUG 22 78			
DEC 22 '79			
AUG 27 1982			
MAY 15			
AUG 20			
AUG 28			
JUN 12			

PUBLIC LIBRARY
SILVERTON, COLO.

BRO
DART   PRINTED IN U.S.A.

Gerald R. Swanson
Box 335
Silverton, Colorado 81433
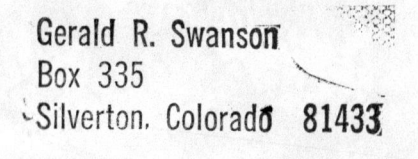

THE HAPPY HOLLISTERS AND THE HAUNTED
HOUSE MYSTERY

The Happy Hollisters
and the
Haunted House Mystery

BY JERRY WEST

Illustrated by Helen S. Hamilton

Doubleday & Company, Inc.

GARDEN CITY, N.Y.

One of the characters in this story is a deaf boy, suggested by a young Irish reader. The author thanks John Andrew Derby of Belfast, Ireland, for the idea, and also acknowledges the help given him by pupils and faculty of the Bruce Street School for the Deaf in Newark, New Jersey.

Copyright © 1962 by Doubleday & Company, Inc.
All Rights Reserved
Printed in the United States of America

Contents

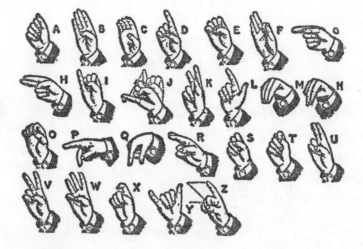

COURTESY OF THE JEWISH SOCIETY FOR THE DEAF.

THE FINGER ALPHABET

CHAPTER 1

THE DETECTIVE CLUB

"THE Shoreham Detective Club will come to order," Pete Hollister said, smiling. At the command of the president, eight children sat down on two benches in the basement playroom of the Hollister home. Pete, twelve, stood before them.

"Secretary Ann Hunter will please call the roll," continued Pete, a blue-eyed boy with a blond crew cut.

Ann read from a large notebook, "Pam Hollister."

"Present," replied Pete's ten-year-old sister.

"Donna Martin."

"Here."

Ann went down the roll. All were present, including the other three Hollister children, Ricky, Holly, and little Sue, and Dave Mead and Jeff Hunter.

"Does anyone have a new mystery to solve?" Pete asked.

"I do," offered Jeff, who was eight. In his hand he held a clipping from the local newspaper. He read, "Ghost hunter wanted to rid a haunted house of spooks. Apply to Mrs. Neeley, 702 Serpentine Road."

"Yikes! That sounds creepy!" red-haired Ricky exclaimed, his freckled face splitting in a grin.

Holly, who was six, a year younger than Ricky, and a tomboy, twirled a brown pigtail. "Let's do it!"

The club members buzzed about the proposed new adventure. Pam had heard about Mrs. Neeley and told the others what she knew. The woman lived on a large estate, situated on the shore of Pine Lake, near the edge of town. On the property was a very old house. It was called the Antique House because it was filled with furnishings dating back to the Civil War.

"Does Mrs. Neeley live there?" asked Donna, who was seven and plump, with a dimple in each cheek.

"No, she doesn't," Pam replied. "Mrs. Neeley lives alone in the gatehouse. It's some distance from the old mansion."

She went on to explain that Mrs. Neeley charged a fee to let people look through the Antique House.

"Yikes, if it's that old," Ricky remarked, "no wonder it's full of spooks!"

"Oh, there are no such things as ghosts," Dave Hunter said. He was Pete's age and the Hollister boy's best friend.

"That's what makes the ad so mysterious," Jeff said. "If there aren't really any ghosts, what is Mrs. Neeley worried about?"

"We'll find that out when we take on the case," Pete replied. "Are there any more questions?"

Someone called "No!" but someone else said "Yes!" and everyone started talking at once.

Little Sue stood up. She was four years old and had jet-black hair cut short with bangs. "Listen to my words," she said loudly.

"Sue has the floor," her big brother announced, trying to hide a smile as he rapped for order.

When everyone was quiet, she asked, "What kind of ant is an antique?"

The other club members laughed and giggled until Pete called for order. Then Pam explained to her little sister that an antique was something very old and usually quite valuable because of its age.

"Oh," Sue said. "Thank you, Pam. Just so long as it isn't one of those big black ants that crawls on my legs sometimes."

"We will now vote on whether to take this case," the club president said formally. "All in favor say——"

Just then there came a loud knock on the door at the top of the stairs which led to the kitchen.

"Yes?" Pete said. "Who is it?"

The door opened and a woman's voice called down cheerily. It was Mrs. Hollister. "Pete," she said, "you have two visitors to your Detective Club."

Pete and Pam exchanged glances. Who could it be? Pete shrugged and replied, "Send them down, please, Mother."

Two pairs of feet clomped down the stairway and in a couple of seconds there stood Joey Brill and his friend Will Wilson.

Joey was Pete's age but larger. He usually wore a frown and had never been friendly with the Hollis-

"Stop that!" Pam said.

ter children. In fact, Joey Brill had played mean tricks on them ever since the family had moved to Shoreham. Dark-haired Will Wilson tagged along after Joey. He did not seem to mind being ordered around by his friend.

"Hello, Joey," Pete said. "Hi, Will."

"Hi," the bigger boy replied, looking a bit uncomfortable. "We heard about your Detective Club and would like to join it."

"We've got a great mystery to solve," put in Will.

"You can't just join our club right off," Pete told them. "You have to pass a test first."

"Like in school?" Joey asked. "Oh no, that's not for us."

Will glanced about the playroom. It was neat and clean. At one end was a ping-pong table, and to the left of it stood a rectangular box. A wire led from it to an electrical outlet in the baseboard.

"What's this?" Joey asked, walking over to the box. He lifted its lid.

"That's a recording machine," Pete replied, going over to the table. "Our whole family has fun with it. Someday we may use it in our detective work."

As Joey started to tinker with the recorder, Will grabbed a table tennis paddle and several of the white balls. He proceeded to bat them against the basement wall.

"Stop that!" Pam said. "You're disturbing our club meeting."

"Can't we have any fun?" Will said, giving his friend a wink. Joey picked up another paddle and he

13

and Will started to bat the ping-pong ball back and forth across the basement floor.

"If you want to play, use the table," Pete suggested, not wishing to act unfriendly to his two callers.

"We don't want to play this silly game anyway," Joey said. "Let's fool with the recorder."

By this time the other club members had risen from their seats and were standing around watching. Joey's rudeness usually ended up in a fight. They all hoped it would not happen here.

"All right," Pete said as he flicked a switch to start the machine. "Joey, why don't you and Will say a few words into the microphone?" The two boys made a couple of remarks and then asked Pete to play them back.

When he heard his own voice, Joey raised his eyebrows in surprise. "I didn't think I sounded like that."

"Pretty dopey, isn't it?" Ricky burst out.

The bully flushed and made a move toward Ricky, but Pete blocked his way.

"We all sound different to others," Pam remarked. Aside to Ricky, she said, "Behave yourself."

"Well, he's breaking up our meeting," Ricky protested.

"All right," Joey said after he and Will had heard their voices. "You can go on with your old meeting. Hey, what's this?" Before Pete could answer, Joey flipped another switch and the recording machine raced in reverse. The noise that came out sounded like ducks quacking fast with high-pitched voices.

All the club members laughed, and when Pete turned off the machine, Holly whispered to Ricky, "It sounded just like Joey and Will."

"Let's get on with the meeting," Pete said as the children returned to their places.

"We'll stand up," Joey told him.

"That's O.K., but be quiet," Pete replied. "We were discussing a new mystery. It's about——"

Joey rudely interrupted by waving his arms. "Say, we've got one that's great. Did you know there was a ghost in Mr. Fundy's cellar?"

"You ought to see it," Will said. "That's the kind of mystery to solve."

Jeff Hunter looked disappointed that the club did not vote immediately on his proposal. Pete merely shrugged. He had to listen as the two intruders rambled on.

Mr. Fundy was an old retired photographer who lived in a small cottage on the far side of Shoreham. He was a tall, angular man with white hair. Pete and Pam had seen him in town several times.

"Mr. Fundy doesn't like kids hanging around his place," Joey said, "but, just the same, the ghost in his cellar needs investigating."

Pete could stand no more of these interruptions. In a loud voice he announced, "This meeting of the Shoreham Detective Club is hereby postponed."

The other members rose, disappointed, and left

the basement by the door which led up into the side yard.

"Not a bad club you've got there," Joey said as they stepped out into the bright sunshine. "Maybe I'll join it—later."

"Me, too," Will added. As the two boys walked toward their bicycles, parked in the driveway near the road, Joey beckoned to Ricky. The red-haired boy walked over to him.

"Wouldn't you like to solve Mr. Fundy's mystery?" Joey asked.

"Sure," Ricky said, "but——"

"But nothing!" Will declared. "The three of us could solve it all by ourselves and be real heroes."

"But I'll do what the club does," Ricky said sternly.

"Oh, I see it now," Joey replied sarcastically. "You're afraid of ghosts."

Ricky's chin thrust out and his mouth tightened.

"There aren't any ghosts, and I'm not afraid of them!" he declared.

"Then come with us to old man Fundy's place," Will said. "The three of us could work together."

Ricky wavered between staying at home or going to the photographer's house to prove he was not afraid.

"O.K.," Ricky said. "I'll go with you, Joey, but no funny business."

When he hastened to the garage to get his bicycle, he saw the rest of the children. They had gone to the back of the big rambling Hollister home, located on the shore of Pine Lake, and were playing down by the water front.

Without stopping to tell them where he was going, Ricky hopped onto his bike, and soon he and the two older boys were pedaling along the shore road toward the opposite side of town. Ten minutes later they came to a little side street, containing only three small bungalows.

"There's Mr. Fundy's place," Joey said, pointing to a house very much in need of a coat of white paint. The screens on the window were rusty, and the grass in the front yard required cutting.

"Where did you see this ghost?" Ricky asked as they parked their bikes at the curb and walked slowly toward the house.

"Around back," Joey whispered. "We saw it through the cellar window."

Bending low to avoid detection, the boys crept around to the rear of the old place. They came to a small window nearly at ground level. The three-paned frame swung into the cellar and was hooked to the ceiling. The screen covering the opening was rusty and had several holes in it.

"Now if you look real close you can see the ghost," Will said.

On hands and knees, Ricky pressed his nose against the screen to get a good look inside. It was dark and gloomy. He could see nothing. Suddenly he felt himself being shoved from behind.

"Hey! Ow!"

Before Ricky could utter another cry, the two boys

had pushed him through the rusty screen. He flew through the air and landed with a thud on a high pile of newspapers under the window. The stack collapsed and Ricky slid to the cellar floor.

CHAPTER 2

A GOOD TURN

RICKY lay breathless for a moment amidst the scattered papers on the wooden floor. After picking himself up, he glanced out the window, a foot over his head. Joey and Will had vanished.

"What'll I do?" he thought as he groped around the dim room. He could see that the walls were lined with cabinets. Each one had several drawers. Ricky wondered what was in them.

"I was foolish to come here," Ricky said to himself. "There isn't any ghost." But no sooner had the thought crossed his mind when he heard a soft, shuffling sound.

The boy did not know which way to turn. There was nothing to hide behind. His only escape could be through the window. Ricky leaped up and grabbed the sill by his finger tips, but he slipped off and landed on the floor again.

The shuffling sounds came closer. "Maybe there is a ghost after all!" he thought frantically. He dared not look back over his shoulder.

Ricky flexed his legs and was about to spring toward the window sill again when suddenly he felt a long bony hand rest on his shoulder.

Too frightened even to scream, he whirled about and looked up into the face of an old man.

"How on earth did you get into here, sonny?" came a kindly voice.

"I—I—I was pushed in," Ricky said honestly, and quickly told the story of how he had been tricked by Joey and Will.

The old man chuckled and reached behind one of the cabinets to flick on a light switch. "Those must be the two rascals I saw prowling around here yesterday," he said.

In the bright light, Ricky was much relieved to see that Mr. Fundy had a pleasant, quizzical, sleepy look on his wrinkled face. His white hair was disheveled, nearly reaching down to his droopy eyelids.

"I was young once and got into mischief myself," he said with a slow smile. "Follow me."

"What are in all these cabinets?" the boy asked as they started up the stairs.

"My life's work, sonny," the old man said. He explained that the cabinets contained negatives of pictures he had taken as far back as fifty years ago.

"Yikes!" Ricky exclaimed. "I guess you lived in ancient times."

Mr. Fundy led the boy to a small living room. In one corner sat an old piano. Across from it was an overstuffed sofa and chair. The walls, Ricky saw immediately, were hung with many faded photographs.

"Thanks for being so nice to me, Mr. Fundy," the boy said. "I'm sorry I snooped around your house without permission."

"Don't mention it," the old gentleman replied. Then he added thoughtfully, "Would you do a favor for me?"

"One good turn deserves another," Ricky said stoutly. "What can I do for you, Mr. Fundy?"

The photographer said he would like several lamb chops from a butcher shop about a quarter of a mile down the road.

"Sure, I'll get 'em for you," Ricky said.

"Charge it to me," the old man told him.

Ricky ran outside, hopped on his bicycle, and pedaled off. He had not gone far when Joey and Will jumped out of some bushes along the road. Their mouths dropped open when they saw Ricky whistling a gay tune.

"Wh—what happened?" Joey asked as he held up his hand to stop the freckle-faced boy.

"You mean after you pushed me?"

Joey looked embarrassed. "Will bumped into me, and I guess I must have bumped into you," he mumbled. "Did you see a ghost down there?"

"I'm not telling you," Ricky declared, "'cause you're not a member of the Detective Club. We keep all our secrets for club members only."

Joey and Will looked enviously at each other.

"Maybe you'd better join the club after all," Will said. "If you can pass the test, perhaps I'll get in, too." Looking very sheepish, Joey hopped on his bike and he and Will raced off.

Ricky went to the butcher and returned to Mr. Fundy's place with a brown bag.

"Here you are, Mr. Fundy," the boy said.

The old man thanked him and tried to press a few coins into his hand.

"Oh no," Ricky protested. "I did that as a favor, Mr. Fundy."

"You sure are a fine lad," the old man said. "If I can ever do you a favor, let me know."

Ricky arrived home in time to see his brothers, sisters, and playmates trooping into the basement to resume their club meeting.

Excitedly, he told them what had happened. "Now Joey and Will want to join the club more than ever," he concluded.

"If they do, we'll have a surprise for them!" Pete exclaimed.

The meeting started quickly and ended soon after the club members voted to apply for the job of ghost hunters at Mrs. Neeley's place.

At the supper table that evening, the children talked over the project with their mother and father. Mrs. Hollister was a slender woman with blue eyes and blond hair. The children's father was a tall, good-looking, well-built man, whose eyes crinkled when he smiled. Mr. Hollister operated The Trading Post in downtown Shoreham. It was a combination hardware store and sports shop which carried a full line of toys.

"You children have solved many cases," Mrs. Hollister said as Pam served her a dessert of apple Betty. "But this sounds like the most mysterious one you've ever tackled."

"I think you'll find that the ghost is only the wind rattling the old house," Mr. Hollister said. "You'll probably clear up the whole thing in no time at all."

"And if you do," the children's mother went on, "perhaps Mrs. Neeley will sell me that old grandfather clock I've often admired."

"Tell me," Mr. Hollister said, "does your Detective Club have a secret code?"

"Not yet," Pete replied. "We'll have to invent one soon."

"It should be something simple," Pam suggested, "so that all of us can learn it quickly."

"Shall it be a written code or should we do it by signs?" Pete asked.

"How about the Indian sign language?" Ricky suggested. He made a motion from his plate to his mouth. "Me big chief. Eatum second dessert!"

"Eatum quick," Pete said as Mrs. Hollister granted her younger son's request. "Mother said Pam and I could go out to see Mrs. Neeley as soon as we all finish helping with the dishes."

When the last plate had been dried and put away, Pete and Pam set off. They pedaled to the other end of town and turned down a twisting lane. In a little while they came to a large property separated from the road by a high fence made of black iron spikes. Behind these stretched a line of dense shrubbery punctuated by tall trees which drooped over the roadway.

Finally they came to a small driveway which led to an open gate. Pete and Pam rode in.

To their right stood a small stone gatehouse. Seated on a lawn chair in front of it was a stout, elderly woman. She wore gold-rimmed glasses and her salt-and-pepper-colored hair was piled high on her head in a large bun.

"We're Pete and Pam Hollister," the boy said. "And we've come to apply for the job as ghost hunters."

Mrs. Neeley lowered her head and peered over the top of her glasses. "Ghost hunters? Such young children?" She paused and added, "Oh yes, I know your mother. She's looked at my antiques several times."

"And she likes your grandfather clock," Pam said with a smile.

"Oh, that clock!" Mrs. Neeley declared. "That's one of the things driving me crazy."

"What's the matter with it?" Pete asked.

"It strikes thirteen," the woman went on, "but only after dark." She shook her finger and said, "It's very dark there at night—no electricity in the old place."

The two children stood astride their bicycles and listened eagerly while she told them of her troubles. "My Antique House has a ghost!" Mrs. Neeley declared so emphatically that her double chin trembled. "And it's frightening away a lot of my business."

"I understand from Mother that you charge admission to see your treasures," Pam said.

"Yes, it's my only source of income," the woman went on. "Now such strange things are happening

"Ghost hunters? Such young children?"

around here that people are afraid to enter the place."
She nodded in the direction of the lake.

The children turned to see a great stone mansion
built in rectangular shape. At each end two tall chim-

neys loomed toward the darkening sky. The Hollisters had often seen it while boating on the lake but had never been this close before.

"What else is spooky besides the clock?" Pete asked.

"Well, there's a spinning wheel," Mrs. Neeley went on. "For some reason it just spins by itself. There are strange lights and sounds, too."

"And tapping on windows, I suppose," Pete said with half a smile.

"Young man, it's not funny," Mrs. Neeley declared, her voice rising with excitement.

"I'm sorry," Pete apologized. "Perhaps it's the wind that's making those sounds, Mrs. Neeley, and tree branches tapping against the window."

"If you'll look clearly, young man," Mrs. Neeley went on, "there's not a tree close enough to the old place."

Pete felt a blush of embarrassment rise to his cheeks. Just because he did not believe in ghosts, the boy thought, did not make it any easier for Mrs. Neeley. It was plain to see that she was upset.

Pam spoke up. "Mrs. Neeley, Pete and I and the Shoreham Detective Club will do all that we can to help solve your mystery—if you'll let us."

Mrs. Neeley's face relaxed into a pleasant smile. "It may be dangerous, and I'd hate to see young folks get into trouble," she said.

"Don't worry, we'll be careful," Pete assured her. As they chatted with the woman, dusk was falling and a light fog was rising from the lake shore and gathering itself around the old stone mansion.

Suddenly Mrs. Neeley gasped. She pointed toward the house. "Look," she said, "there it is!"

"What?" Pete asked as he whirled about.

"That light. See it?"

In a third-floor dormer window near the chimney a dim light flickered on and off. Pete and Pam looked on wide-eyed. Their spines tingled as they heard a low moaning sigh drift through the quiet evening from the direction of the old mansion.

CHAPTER 3

JOEY'S INITIATION

As PETE and Pam watched, the light in the window blinked on and off once more. Then the moaning dropped to a whisper and stopped.

"Now will you believe me?" Mrs. Neeley asked the two children.

"There must be someone in there," Pete said.

"Have you notified the police department, Mrs. Neeley?"

The woman replied that she had done this when the ghostly happenings had begun about a month before. "But the police have been of no help to me," she went on. "They searched the house in the day-time and also at night but could find nothing."

"May we take a look around?" Pete asked.

"I've already locked the house for the night," Mrs. Neeley said, "and I wouldn't go up there now for anything! But you can look around outside."

After thanking her, the Hollisters parked their bicycles alongside the gatehouse and walked toward the old mansion.

"We'd better hurry, Pam," Pete said, "before it gets too dark to see anything."

Suddenly the brother and sister were startled by a rabbit which hopped across the path in front of them.

"Oh!" Pam exclaimed.

Her brother chuckled. "Rabbits can't hurt us, but I think there's something more dangerous than bunnies in that old mansion."

Now the place loomed up before them, a dark mass against the blue-black evening sky.

Pete and Pam stopped and listened. Silence.

Bending low to conceal themselves behind bushes, the two children cautiously circled the big place. An owl hooted in the distance, but otherwise the woods around the Antique House were quiet.

Pete whispered to his sister. "If someone was inside the house he might be on his way out. Let's hide beside the front door and wait for a few minutes."

Two tall thick boxwood hedges flanked the oak door at the front of the mansion. Pete and Pam quietly pushed their way into the shrubs.

"I think I hear something," Pam whispered after a few seconds.

The boy strained his ears, listening. Now he heard the sound, too. It was like a heavy door creaking.

As Pete peered through the foliage, his heart pounded wildly. The front door opened slowly about six inches. But nobody came out.

Now came the noise of shuffling, as if a person were walking across the floor. Then they heard thumping, which grew fainter.

"Someone's climbing stairs," Pam said as the sound died out in the distance.

"Let's go in and take a look," Pete suggested, although he was not really sure he wanted to.

"Oh no," his sister replied. "It might be a trap to catch us! Besides, we don't have any flashlight."

"I guess you're right. Let's go. I'm going to tell Officer Cal about this the first thing in the morning."

Pete stepped out of his hiding place in the boxwood hedge, but Pam tugged at his hand.

"I can't move!" she whispered. "My ankle's stuck."

Pete reached down and felt his sister's foot. It was tightly wedged between two stout branches of boxwood.

As he worked to free her, a soft glow suddenly covered them. The two children glanced up in amazement to see the light again in the same dormer window on the top floor.

"Oh, Pete, hurry!" Pam cried.

Using both hands, the boy tugged at her ankle. The thumping sounds started again, this time getting louder as they came closer.

"There!" Pete exclaimed as he pulled his sister's foot free.

"My shoe came off!" Pam exclaimed.

"Come on!" Pete urged. "We'll get it later!"

The two youngsters raced back to the gatehouse. Mrs. Neeley was waiting where they had left her.

"I thought the mosquitoes would get me before you returned," she said.

"I thought something else would get us," Pete re-

"What's all the excitement?"

marked ruefully. "Mrs. Neeley, you really have trouble in that old mansion."

"But we'll try to help you," Pam assured her kindly.

The two children said good-by, turned on their bicycle lights, and pedaled home.

When Pam limped into the living room without her shoe, everybody wanted to know what had happened. Pete told them the story. "It'll be a real job for our Detective Club," he concluded.

"You'll be wise to discuss your case with Officer Cal," their mother said as the children started upstairs to bed.

Shortly after breakfast the next morning, Pam telephoned their policeman friend. He told her he planned to cruise their area in the police car and would drop by the house.

Pete was mowing the lawn and the other children were helping their mother weed the flower bed when Officer Cal pulled into the driveway. He was a handsome young man with ruddy cheeks and clear blue eyes. In the past he had helped the Hollisters, and they had helped him to solve several mysteries.

When Officer Cal stepped out of the car, little Sue raced to him. He scooped her up in his arms and put his policeman's hat on her head.

"What's all the excitement, Pam?" he asked as the children gathered around him.

"It's about Mrs. Neeley's Antique House," the

girl replied. "She thinks it's haunted and wants us to find the ghost."

Officer Cal set Sue down. The little girl marched off to show her mother the hat. The policeman ran a hand through his hair and half smiled. "You don't really believe there's a ghost, do you?"

"Of course not," Pete answered. "But there's something spooky going on at that place."

"Officer Cal, maybe there *is* a ghost," Holly said.

"Yikes, you can't be too sure about a place that old," Ricky chimed in.

Much to the amazement of the Hollister children, the policeman told them of a rumor that Mrs. Neeley was haunting her own house in order to gain publicity.

"Oh, I just don't believe that!" Pam declared. "She's such a nice old lady."

Officer Cal shrugged. "We've searched the place, you know."

"And found nothing," Pete said. "Mrs. Neeley told us about that."

Then Pam related what had happened to them the night before. When Officer Cal got a skeptical look in his eye, she was disappointed.

Noticing this, the policeman said, "Well, all right, Pam. Show me where you hid in the hedge and I'll get the shoe for you."

"And if it isn't there," Pete said, "then what?"

"Then I'll believe there's a ghost in the old Antique House," Officer Cal replied with a chuckle.

At that moment Sue returned with a snapdragon

pinned to Officer Cal's hat. "Here's a present from Mommy," the little girl said, and Mrs. Hollister waved to the officer.

"May I take the children on a short ride?" the policeman called out.

When their mother laughed and said yes, the five youngsters squeezed into the squad car. Pete and Pam sat in front, while Ricky, Holly, and Sue occupied the rear seat.

On the way to 702 Serpentine Road, Officer Cal passed Joey and Will on their bicycles. The bullies looked amazed to see the Hollisters riding in the police car.

Mrs. Neeley, who was sitting at her window, was surprised to see Officer Cal and all the children pull up in front of the gatehouse.

"Have you had any visitors yet today?" Pam asked her as she came out to greet them.

"No, it's a little too early," the woman replied.

Then Officer Cal spoke up. "I'd like to look in the boxwood hedge near the front door, Mrs. Neeley. Pam lost a shoe there last night."

"Go right ahead," Mrs. Neeley said.

Ricky, Holly, and Sue stayed to chat with the woman while Pete and Pam strode off with the policeman toward the mansion.

"There's the hedge," Pete said, pointing.

"We were hiding in the middle of it," Pam explained, "when we heard the thumping and saw the light."

"Here's the exact spot," Pete added, stooping beside it.

With strong hands, Officer Cal parted the branches.

Pam's shoe had vanished.

"Crickets!" Pete exclaimed, and gulped.

The officer turned to the children, a serious expression on his face. "There *is* something funny going on here," he said. "I'm sorry I doubted you."

As they walked back to the gatehouse, the policeman told them that he was very busy working on another case but that he would assist the children all that he could in solving their mystery.

"Can you tell us about yours?" Pam asked.

Officer Cal explained that he was trying to clear up jewelry thefts which had been going on in Shoreham and the area around it for several months.

"I hope you catch the thief," Pam said.

"And I hope you catch your ghost," he replied, smiling.

When they reached the gatehouse, Pete and Pam saw Mrs. Neeley rocking in gales of laughter.

"Oh, this little girl!" Mrs. Neeley gasped, putting a plump arm around Sue.

"Sue was naughty," Holly said. "She asked Mrs. Neeley if she was an antique, too."

The woman enjoyed the joke on herself so much that everyone smiled, including Officer Cal.

In a few moments the children said good-by, and soon they were back home.

"Keep in touch with me," Officer Cal said as he drove off.

A few minutes later Joey and Will rode their bicycles into the yard.

"Hey, Pete!" Joey called out. "If I join your Detective Club, will I get to ride in the police car, too?"

"Perhaps," Pete answered. "Are you willing to be initiated?"

"What's that for?" the boy asked, scowling.

"To show how brave you are," Pete replied. "Detectives can't be frightened, you know."

When Joey said he would take the test, the Hollisters told him to come back late in the afternoon.

"I'll see how Joey makes out," Will said. "Then I'll join later."

When the two friends had pedaled off, Pam quickly telephoned the other club members.

Right after lunch all of them except little Sue, who was taking a nap, sat under a large willow tree near the Hollisters' dock on the edge of Pine Lake.

"Let's make this an initiation Joey won't ever forget!" Dave Mead said.

Pete, sitting cross-legged, plucked a long blade of grass and chewed on it thoughtfully. "What shall we do with him?"

"Scare him!" Ricky demanded.

"But not too much," Pam said. "He might get nightmares."

"I don't think Joey will scare too easily," Ann Hunter said.

"I think he will," replied her brother Jeff.

Pete snapped his fingers. "I know what we'll do," he said. "But we'll need a few things. Jeff, suppose you bring your pet duck; and Dave, can you get that plastic skull that you used last Halloween?"

"Sure thing."

"What can I bring?" Donna Martin asked.

"Well," Pete told her, "We'll need some cold spaghetti."

"Good!" Donna giggled. "Mother has some left over from last night's supper."

"Pam, Ricky, Holly, and I will take care of the sound effects and lights," Pete went on. "Let's all meet in our basement in half an hour."

"Let's go!" Dave said. He scrambled to his feet and raced off to his house, a few doors down the road.

Joey Brill arrived at the Hollister home at four o'clock. Will Wilson, looking anxious, waited outside while his friend rapped on the screen door.

Mrs. Hollister greeted him. "The children are waiting for you in the playroom, Joey. This way, please." She led him to the kitchen and opened the cellar door.

The boy started down the steps. When he reached the bottom the light suddenly snapped off.

"Hey, what's going on here?" he cried, groping in the darkness. All the cellar windows had been covered with black cloth so that no light came in at all.

His foot found the first step, and he was going to

retreat when a voice said hollowly, "Joey, your initiation is about to begin." There was an eerie wailing sound and a clanking of chains.

"Who—who said that?" the boy asked.

A small light flicked on, throwing a beam across an eerie white skull. The jaw moved up and down as the voice continued. "This is a simple test of your bravery, Joey Brill. Reach out your right hand."

The boy did so. His fingers touched the rim of a bowl and slipped in to feel something cold and stringy.

"Eat it!" came the voice, and there were several snickers in the darkness.

"They're wo-worms!" Joey said timorously. "I ca-can't eat them!"

"You must!"

Joey pretended to do so and said, "All right, what's next?"

"The snake pit," came the hollow voice as the jaw of the skull moved up and down.

The voice directed Joey to proceed to the center of the basement, where a carton rested upon a table. With a click another flashlight beam shone upon the box.

"It is filled with deadly cobras and rattlers," the voice said again. "Put your hand in and get them!"

"Hah, you can't fool me," Joey said. He stepped up to the box gingerly and saw that there was a small round hole cut into the top.

"Reach in!" the voice commanded again.

Gathering up all his courage, Joey thrust his hand into the hole.

"Ow! The snake bit me!" Joey cried in terror. He ran to the steps, half fell up them, and, with a mad dash, flew out of the front door.

CHAPTER 4

A CURIOUS STRANGER

THE screen door slammed. Joey Brill cleared the Hollisters' front steps in one leap and took off like a gazelle, with Will Wilson running behind him.

When they reached the street both boys stopped and examined Joey's right hand. Then they ran off.

Seeing this from a window, Mrs. Hollister called down the basement steps, "Pete, what did you do to Joey? He looked so pale!"

"He got nipped by Jeff's duck."

"Why, you'd think he was bitten by a sidewinder the way he tore out of here."

The children laughed, and Dave Mead said, "He failed to pass the test. He's not a member of our Detective Club."

By the next morning the story of Joey's scare had spread among the youngsters of Shoreham. A fourteen-year-old boy passed him on the street, grinned, and said, "Quack, quack!"

"I'll get even with those Hollisters," Joey muttered to himself. But for a while the bully's embarrassment caused him to stay away from their neighborhood.

With Joey gone, the Detective Club was free to carry on its work without interruption.

That afternoon Pete, Pam, Ricky, and Holly, along with Jeff, Ann, Dave, and Donna, rode their bicycles to the Antique House.

Mrs. Neeley said that they might look around until customers arrived. She asked that the children step outside while the sight-seers browsed about the old place.

"Of course, Mrs. Neeley," Pam replied. "We'll be glad to do that."

"And please be careful of my antiques," the stout woman cautioned them as they started walking up the wide drive to the mansion.

"Why don't you girls look around inside while we fellows scout the property?" Pete suggested when they reached the front door. "If you get into any trouble, holler," he added as the girls entered the Antique House. Then he turned to Dave, Jeff, and Ricky. "Let's look for footprints."

The four circled the stone mansion. Pete parted the bushes and examined the ground beneath the first-floor windows. There was no sign of anyone's having stood beneath them.

The boys proceeded in ever-widening circles, getting farther and farther from the house. But they discovered no footprints or any other clues.

Finally they found themselves on the shore front. "This is as far as we can go," Dave said. "Shucks. No luck."

They decided to join the girls inside the Antique

House. Ricky ran on ahead. As he rounded the corner of the stone mansion he stopped short and held up his right hand. Pete, Jeff, and Dave raced to his side.

"What's up?" Pete asked.

"Somebody's spying on us."

"Where?" Jeff asked, scanning the property as far as the iron picket fence.

"Over there, under that tree." Ricky pointed to a huge beech whose branches were so low that they nearly touched the ground.

Pete could plainly see a man's trousers, but the rest of the fellow was concealed in the foliage.

"Do you suppose he's seen us?" Dave asked.

"We'll soon know," Pete said. "Come on. Follow me."

Making their way quietly in single file like four Indians, the boys retreated toward the shore until they were hidden in a thicket; then they made a wide circuit until their path followed the iron fence.

"Quiet now," Pete warned them as they crept up toward the beech tree, keeping out of sight behind bushes.

"There he is," Pete said.

The man was in plain view now. He was gazing at the entrance of the Antique House. He held a small piece of paper in the palm of his hand and kept glancing at it and then at the old mansion.

"What's he up to?" Dave whispered.

"Yikes! He isn't very big," Ricky said in a low voice. "Let's catch him! He may be the ghost we're looking for!"

"We have no reason to do that," Pete said. "He isn't doing anything unlawful."

Pete examined the man long and hard, taking in every detail. He was short and wiry and had black hair closely plastered to his head. His nose was long and thin. The fellow wore slacks and a sports shirt with the sleeves rolled up, revealing muscular arms.

"Let's try asking him some questions," Pete said. The boy stepped out from behind a forsythia bush and called to the man. "Hello there! I'd like to speak to you a moment."

The stranger turned his head, and a look of surprise and embarrassment came over his face. Without a word he turned, ran to the picket fence, and scaled it with the ease of a cat.

"Yikes! Look at him go!" Ricky exclaimed. "He's our man all right!"

The boys tore after him, but before they could even reach the fence they heard the sound of a motor scooter and realized that their quarry had gone.

As the boys walked back to the old mansion, Dave said, "He acted as if he was trying to find something."

"Yes. He didn't look like a criminal," Pete remarked, "but he sure didn't want to be questioned."

The four boys determined to be on the lookout for the curious stranger. They had nearly reached the front entrance to the mansion when Holly poked her head out the door and cried, "Hurry! Pam wants you!"

When Pete dashed inside, he was amazed at the huge living room he had entered. It was almost the width of the house, and a balcony ran along three sides of it.

Pete glanced up to see Pam, Ann, and Donna looking at an old spinning wheel. He raced up the stairs to where they stood. Ricky, Jeff, and Dave followed.

"Crickets! I thought you were in trouble," the blond-haired boy said.

"Mrs. Neeley was right," Pam remarked. "Look at this spinning wheel, Pete."

Her brother glanced at it. It seemed to be just like other spinning wheels he had seen. But suddenly there was a strange humming sound and the wheel slowly began to turn.

"Wow! Would you look at that!" Dave cried out.

The boys got down on hands and knees and examined the antique carefully. There were no wires to be seen or any hidden gear that might cause the movement.

"Maybe when the ghost hums a tune the spinning starts," Jeff said, bewildered.

The noise stopped and so did the wheel.

"See, I told you so," the younger boy said shakily. "This place is really haunted."

"Where's Holly?" Pam asked suddenly. They all looked around. The pig-tailed girl was missing.

A moment later they heard her scream from somewhere above. There was a crashing sound, then several loud bumps.

"Holly! Where are you?" Pam cried as she raced toward the staircase which led upward.

When she reached it, Pam saw her sister sprawled

halfway down. A small scatter rug was draped over one shoulder. "I was exploring," Holly said, "and slipped."

"This place makes me nervous," Donna said as she, Ann, and Pam helped Holly to her feet and replaced the rug at the top of the stairs.

Footsteps sounded on the main floor as several visitors came to look at the antiques. Keeping their promise to Mrs. Neeley, the children hastened to the gatehouse. After telling what had happened, they thanked her and were mounting their bikes to go home when two women hurried from the Antique House. Their faces were ashen gray.

"Give us our money back!" one of them demanded. "Why, your spinning wheel . . ."

"Poor Mrs. Neeley," Holly said sadly as they set off. "We must solve her mystery quickly, Pete. Otherwise she won't have any money."

On the way home the girls reported that they had also searched the old cellar.

"What did you find?" Ricky asked.

"Nothing exciting," Ann replied. "Several little rooms. One had a fireplace."

Jeff, Ann, Dave, and Donna reached their homes first. The Hollisters continued on to their own place, with Pete last in the line of bicycles.

The other three skipped into the house to tell of their adventure while Pete put his bike in the garage. As he stepped out, a movement by the road caught his eye. He saw a small man staring at the Hollisters' home.

"I was exploring and slipped," said Holly.

It was the same person who had scaled Mrs. Neeley's iron fence!

The man glanced at something in his hand, then at the house. Quietly Pete remounted his bicycle. He pedaled out to the drive, calling, "Wait! I want to talk to you!"

Ignoring the plea, the man hurried off. As Pete took after him he broke into a swift run and cut through an empty lot across the street. The boy wondered where his motor scooter was.

Suddenly the fugitive zigzagged into a patch of woods.

"Stop!" Pete called out.

The man darted from one tree to another, neatly eluding his pursuer. In a moment he had outdistanced Pete and disappeared, but the boy kept pedaling, looking this way and that.

Suddenly he spotted a motor scooter resting against a big boulder.

But before he could stop his bicycle, the front wheel hit a rock and he sailed over the handle bars. His head banged into a tree. Pete blacked out for a moment and lay motionless.

Then his eyes fluttered open. As he looked up into the branches he said to himself, "Am I dreaming?"

The fugitive was swinging down from limb to limb. He finally dropped to the ground beside the amazed lad.

CHAPTER 5

A NEW MYSTERY

PETE lay still, looking up in disbelief at the wiry little man. The fellow knelt beside him. "Are you all right?" he asked.

Pete struggled to his feet. "Who are you?" he asked. "And what were you doing spying on our house?"

The man's boyish face looked shy and embarrassed. "It's a long story," he said, "and I hope you'll believe me."

"I'll listen," Pete replied. "There are some questions you must answer, Mr. ———"

"Kerry Flip is my name," the stranger said. "I'm an acrobat and have an act at the carnival in the State Park."

"Kerry Flip," Pete said, repeating the name. "It's an odd one. Is it because you do flip-flops in your work?"

"That's right," the man replied. "I don't know my real name. That's why I'm doing these things that seem mysterious to you."

Pete brushed himself off, picked up his bicycle, and stood it against the tree. As he did, Kerry Flip pulled a small photograph from his pocket.

"I'm trying to solve a mystery," he said, handing the photo to Pete.

It showed a little old-fashioned girl about Holly's age. She was standing next to an ornate doorway of an old house. Beside the threshold was a boot scraper shaped like an elephant with a flat back.

Pete studied the picture carefully. It looked as if it might have been cut off from a larger photograph.

"Who is it?" the boy asked.

"That little girl was my mother," came the acrobat's reply. "I'm trying to trace my family."

"Your family?" Pete asked, looking perplexed.

"I know it sounds funny to you," Kerry Flip went on, "but I don't know who I really am. How would you like that?"

Pete just shook his head. It was good to know that he was Pete Hollister, and he told the acrobat so.

"Maybe I could help you," the boy said. "Our family likes to solve mysteries."

"Good," Kerry replied. "I'll tell you the whole story."

He and Pete seated themselves on the grass under the tree. Kerry Flip spun the strangest tale that Pete had ever heard.

The acrobat's earliest memories went back to when he was four years old. He was traveling with his mother and father through the cities of Europe doing a tumbling act.

"We were known as The Three Flips," Kerry said. "My father came from Switzerland and my mother was an American. But neither of them would ever tell

49

me what our real name was or anything about the family."

"Why?" Pete asked.

"I don't know," Kerry said, shaking his head. "Maybe they were ashamed of something in the past. My father died when I was sixteen and my mother became ill shortly afterward."

Pete was now fascinated by this strange story. "What does this have to do with your spying on our house and Mrs. Neeley's place?" he asked.

Kerry heaved a sigh and went on. "Before my mother died," he said, "she pressed this picture into my hands, saying that it was taken in Shoreham. She promised to tell me the mystery of my family the next day. But by then it was too late."

"I'm sorry," Pete said.

"That was long ago," Kerry replied. "I continued with my act and traveled all over the world. When I found myself in Shoreham last week, I was determined to find out who I was."

"Now I see!" Pete exclaimed. "You were looking at all the old houses to find this particular doorway."

"Yes," Kerry answered. "If I could only find the house where my mother used to live, I might learn more about her."

"I hope you do," Pete said earnestly.

The acrobat said that between acts at the State Park he had gone to look at many old houses in Shoreham, but nowhere could he find the ornate doorway. "Have you ever seen one like it?" he asked.

Pete studied the photo in detail. At the bottom was

a stone step, on which the girl stood. Over the doorway was an arch decorated with an eagle's head.

"No, I've never seen anything like this," Pete confessed. "It certainly is odd."

"That's why I thought it would be easy to locate," Kerry said.

"But why did you run away from us?" Pete asked.

Kerry told him that he was naturally a shy person and did not want others to know what he was doing.

"I thought people might laugh if they knew I was searching for old doorways," the acrobat said, looking squarely into Pete's eyes.

"Let me help you," Pete said, and told Kerry about the Shoreham Detective Club. The boy said that if the man would let him have the photo, he would have copies made and give one to every club member. "In that way," Pete said, "we can all be looking for the old doorway."

At first Kerry was reluctant to give up the important clue. Finally he said, "I know I can trust you, Pete. But be very careful of it. If you lose this picture I may never find out who I really am."

Pete promised to take extra care of the old photo. Before they parted, he learned that Kerry was staying at the Lake Motel near the State Park.

"I'll let you know what we find," the boy said. He added, "When you come to town, drop in and say hello to us."

The acrobat drove off on his motor scooter and Pete rode his bike home.

At supper that evening everyone discussed the strange story of Kerry Flip.

"The Detective Club certainly has its share of new mysteries to solve," Mrs. Hollister remarked.

"You're right," Pam said. "I'd like to help Mr. Flip."

"Maybe we could go out and see him do his act," Ricky declared. It was decided that first they should hold another club meeting to discuss their new case.

The members were called together the next morning in their basement clubroom. Everyone was keenly interested in finding the old doorway.

"Since we have two mysteries on our hands," Pete said, "I recommend that the younger members of our club take charge of Kerry Flip's case."

Ricky, Holly, Donna, and Jeff Hunter exchanged excited glances.

"We'd love to!" Holly said. "What can we do first, Pete?"

"Have copies made of this picture," he said, handing it to Holly. "Go to the photo shop near Dad's store."

While the older children remained to talk about the haunted house mystery, Ricky, Holly, Donna, and Jeff hopped on their bicycles and set off for town.

The photo shop, run by Mr. Akers, was down the street from The Trading Post. The four children rode through the alley alongside Mr. Hollister's building and parked in back of his store. Then they set off on foot for Mr. Aker's shop.

As they passed the window of the photo shop, Jeff stopped to look at the display. "Those are keen movie cameras," he said.

"Look at them for a while if you want," Holly told him. "The rest of us'll go inside."

Mr. Akers, a man about their father's age, looked at the picture the pig-tailed girl gave him. "You say you want a copy of this?" he asked.

"Eight copies, if you please," Holly replied.

Mr. Akers cocked his head to one side and looked at them with a smile. "Is this another mystery you children are solving?"

"We wouldn't like to say," Holly answered.

" 'Cause it's a secret," Donna added.

"For our Detective Club," Ricky spoke up proudly. "That's all we can tell you, Mr. Akers."

"All right," the man said. "The prints will be ready in a couple of days."

The children thanked the man and stepped outside the store. Jeff Hunter stood there with his hands in his pockets, looking after Joey Brill, who was walking off down the street.

"Was he bothering you?" Ricky asked.

"No," Jeff said. "Joey saw you go into the store and wondered what you were doing."

"You didn't tell him?" Holly asked.

Jeff looked embarrassed. "Well, yes, I told him a little bit. I didn't think it would hurt."

"But you weren't supposed to!" Holly protested. "Good detectives keep secrets."

"Golly, I'm sorry," Jeff said. "Joey seemed so friendly today."

"He's always like that when he's up to something," Ricky said.

"All right, I won't do it again," Jeff promised. He said good-by to the others and went home to do an errand for his mother.

After Donna had skipped off to the Soda Shoppe down the street, Ricky and Holly headed for The Trading Post to see their father. As they stepped inside the large modern store, Mr. Hollister hurried up the center aisle to greet them.

"I was hoping one of you children would drop in," he said, putting his arms around Ricky and Holly. "I have an errand at the bank and need someone to mind the store while I'm gone."

"Yikes, that'll be keen," Ricky said.

Left alone, he and Holly glanced about proudly at the hardware, toys, and sporting goods.

"I'm going to have a store like this myself some-day," the boy said.

"Look," Holly remarked. "Here comes a customer."

Through the front door came a short, dark-haired man. Ricky threw out his chest and walked up to the customer. "Is there something I can do for you, sir?" he asked, imitating his father.

The man glanced down at the small boy. "You look like Pete Hollister. You must be his brother."

"And I'm his sister," Holly said, walking over.

"I'm Kerry Flip," the man said, "and I want——"

"Kerry Flip!" the children chorused.

"Our Detective Club is trying to solve your mystery!" Ricky said excitedly.

"Thank you," the acrobat said. "Do you have any——"

"It must be great to be a tumbler," Holly said, "and travel all over the world!"

"We're going to see your act someday," Ricky said, grinning. Then he looked very serious. "You didn't tell us what you wanted, Mr. Flip."

The man chuckled. "I'd like to buy a piece of rope."

"Rope. Hmmm," Ricky said. "Is it for a clothesline or a lasso or——"

"Or skipping?" Holly asked.

"No," the acrobat replied. "It's for my act. I need new rope for my flying rings. Do you have stout Manila hemp?"

Ricky did not know for certain, but he led Kerry Flip to the back of the store, where his father kept rope on huge wooden spools.

"There's the kind I want," the man said as he examined a sturdy coil of hemp.

"How much do you need?" Ricky asked him.

"Thirty feet."

The two children measured off the desired length and Ricky snipped it with a pair of large shears.

As the price of the rope was written on the spool, Kerry Flip had no difficulty paying the correct amount.

"I'm an acrobat!"

When he left the store, Ricky said, "Why don't we get some rope and make a flying ring?"

"But we don't have any ring," Holly said.

"We can make a loop in the rope," Ricky replied. "Come on, let's do it."

Ricky cut a long piece of rope. Then, standing on a stepladder, he tied one end to a pipe crossing the ceiling of The Trading Post. Holly helped him fasten a loop. Next, Ricky grasped the loop in both his hands and swung to and fro.

"Ha, I'm an acrobat!" he called out.

"Let me try it, too," Holly said.

After giving her a turn, Ricky declared, "I've got a keener idea."

"What's that?"

"I'll show you," Ricky said, and climbed the ladder again. This time he put one foot through the loop. Holding the rope with his hands, he swung back and forth over the display counters.

But suddenly Ricky cried out. His hands slipped from the rope. He zoomed through the air, dangling by one leg.

"Help! Help!" Holly cried, and ran to the front of the store. She nearly collided with her father, who was entering at that very moment.

"Ricky's stuck!" Holly cried out. Mr. Hollister hastened to where his son was dangling like a rag doll on a string. Standing on the ladder, he quickly untied the knot and released him.

"You can't sell things upside down, Ricky," his father said. "What kind of a salesman is that?"

The boy grinned sheepishly, said he was sorry, and told about the sale they had made to Kerry Flip.

"All right, Acrobat Ricky," his father said with a wink. "You can go home now and tumble around the yard." He kissed them good-by before they set off.

As they rode along a shady street not far from where they lived, Ricky and Holly came up behind a boy walking on the sidewalk. Then suddenly, as if from nowhere, Joey Brill flashed past them, his bicycle wheels humming.

"Dang-dang, gangway!"

The boy kept straight ahead.

"Scram!" Joey screamed. With that his front wheel struck the boy, knocking him head over heels.

CHAPTER 6

FINGER ALPHABET

HOLLY and Ricky ran to the boy who had been knocked down. As they helped him to his feet they saw that his left elbow was skinned and bleeding.

Joey, meanwhile, circled his bicycle around to look at the results of his mischief.

"You're a meanie!" Holly scolded.

"Why did you do that, Joey!" Ricky cried out. "He wasn't hurting you."

The boy, about twelve, was slender and had brown hair and eyes. He looked pleadingly at Holly and Ricky but said nothing.

Joey only smirked. "He's a new kid in town. I wanted to show him who's boss!"

"You didn't have to run into him!" Ricky retorted.

"I warned him," Joey answered. "What more does he want?"

"You're just a big bully, and I'm going to tell Pete," Ricky went on, shaking his fist.

Joey rode close to the red-haired boy and slapped him as he went by. Then he pedaled fast and disappeared down the street.

"He's angry because he couldn't join our Detective

Club," Holly remarked to the injured boy. For the first time she realized that he was watching her closely as she spoke.

"What's your name?" Ricky asked.

The lad opened his mouth but only high-pitched, slurred sounds came out.

"I can't understand you," Holly said.

The boy repeated the words, but still they were not clear. Then he pulled a pad and pencil from his pocket and wrote on it:

My name is Charles Belden. I am deaf.

Holly and Ricky were stunned. No wonder he did not get out of the way of Joey's bicycle. He did not hear him coming!

"Oh, I'm sorry," Holly said. "Can you understand me?"

Both children listened extra carefully to Charles' reply. The words were still high-pitched and indistinct, but now they could understand. "Yes," was the answer; "I read lips."

"Come with us," Holly said, "and we'll fix your skinned elbow."

Charles nodded and walked along in silence with his two new friends. His eyes grew wide with delight when he saw the Hollisters' home.

Pete and Pam were in the shade of the garage, giving two lawn chairs a coat of white paint. Holly and Ricky wheeled their bikes up the drive and quickly introduced the new boy.

"Hello," Charles said in his strange-sounding voice.

"We're so sorry you're hurt," Pam told him. "Come in the house. Mother and I will take care of you."

Pete and Pam put down their brushes, removed their paint gloves, and led Charles Belden into their living room. Mrs. Hollister was watering a pot of African violets on a table near a window, while Sue played on the floor with her doll. The children's mother set down her copper watering can and hastened to examine the boy's elbow.

While introductions were still being made, Mrs. Hollister, followed by Sue, took Charles to the bathroom, where she bathed his wound, applied antiseptic, and bandaged it. Then they took their guest to the front porch, where they all sat down to talk.

"Where do you live?" Mrs. Hollister asked Charles.

"And where do you come from?" Ricky inquired.

"How long have you been deaf?" was Holly's question.

"Please, children," their mother said. "Charles can't read all of our lips at once."

The deaf boy took the paper and pencil from his pocket and began to write carefully. When he finished, he held the note smilingly toward Mrs. Hollister. It said that Charles was from the city, where he lived with his mother, father, and grandfather. He was spending the summer at the Johnson farm, helping the farmer in return for a vacation in the country. He had been born without his hearing and attended a school for the deaf in the city.

Mr. Johnson, the Hollisters knew, operated a farm adjoining Shoreham. He raised vegetables and also had a few goats.

Being new to the area, Charles had walked in to see Shoreham and was on his way back to the Johnson farm when Joey's bike hit him.

The Hollisters had never known a deaf child before. Charles looked from one face to another as the brothers and sisters spoke to him. He smiled and directed a remark to Pam. "I understand you best," he said. She was delighted at being able to make out his words. While the other children made exaggerated motions with their lips, Pam spoke slowly and naturally.

Mrs. Hollister asked Charles to stay for lunch. When he smiled happily and said he would, Holly scampered to set another place and Pam offered to call the farmer's wife so that she would not worry about him.

Charles enjoyed the lunch of sandwiches, lemonade, and chocolate cake. By the time they had finished eating, all the Hollisters were beginning to understand him when he spoke. They looked sorry when he said slowly, "I must go."

"Come back soon," their mother told him.

"How about tomorrow!" Pam suggested. "Maybe we can have a picnic after church."

"Crickets!" Pete exclaimed. "That would be great fun. We could invite Kerry Flip, too."

"That would be nice," Mrs. Hollister said. She added, "Charles, I'll drive you to the farm. Come."

The children's father had taken The Trading Post delivery truck that morning, leaving the station wagon in the driveway. As everyone climbed in, Sue insisted on sitting next to Charles.

They set off for the Johnson farm, and when they arrived Pam wrote a note so that the deaf boy would be sure to understand. It said, *We will call for you at one o'clock tomorrow.*

Charles' face brightened. He nodded vigorously and said in his odd voice, "Thank you. Good-by, good-by."

"I feel so sorry for Charles," Pam remarked as they drove home again.

"He's a bright, kind boy," Mrs. Hollister said. "He reads lips very well and will be a fine and useful person in spite of his handicap."

"Yikes!" Ricky said. "Better than Joey Brill."

"Joey didn't realize he was deaf," Mrs. Hollister replied as they pulled into their driveway. "I'm sure he'll feel sorry when he learns it."

When she stepped out of the car, Pam heard their telephone ringing and ran to answer it.

The caller was Mrs. Neeley. "Is this Pam?" she asked.

"Yes, it is."

"Thank you, children! Thank you so much!" came the woman's voice.

"What did we do?" Pam asked.

"You rid my Antique House of the ghost, that's what," she replied.

Mrs. Neeley went on to say that there were no

groans or strange noises in the old mansion that day. Even the spinning wheel behaved, and her visitors had not been disturbed.

"Come and see me sometime tomorrow," the woman went on, "and I will give you and your club a reward for your services."

Pam put down the phone in stunned silence. The mystery solved? And so easily? What had they done to chase the ghost? If a mysterious intruder had been responsible for the mischief, why had he departed so suddenly?

When Pam told Pete about the call, her brother scratched his head in disbelief. "I think the ghost is lying low for some reason," Pete said. "We haven't heard the end of him yet."

"But if the Antique House trouble is over," Pam remarked, "we'll have more time to spend on Kerry Flip's mystery."

"Let's phone him right now," Pete suggested, "and invite him over with Charles tomorrow afternoon."

Kerry was reached at the Lake Motel. He said that he had a performance at four o'clock next afternoon but would be happy to drop in after the children had returned from church.

At one o'clock sharp next day Mrs. Hollister and the children called for Charles Belden at the Johnson farm. His trousers were pressed, his shirt freshly ironed, and his hair combed neatly.

"You can always tell when it's Sunday," Ricky remarked as the deaf boy stepped into the car.

They arrived home to find Kerry Flip's motor scooter sitting beside the garage. The acrobat was on the porch talking with Mr. Hollister. When the family trooped up the steps, the two guests were introduced.

"Charles is deaf," Pam explained, "but he can read lips."

The acrobat shook hands with the boy and said, "I worked with a deaf performer once. He was always seeing things out of the corners of his eyes that the rest of us missed." Then Kerry explained, "That's because people without hearing develop excellent side vision."

Smiling at Charles, Kerry began to make rapid movements with his right fist and fingers. The boy beamed and did the same.

Seeing the amazed looks on the Hollisters' faces, Kerry said, "We're talking with the finger alphabet. I learned it years ago." He explained that most schools for the deaf teach only lip reading. "Many pupils who are twelve or more learn either the sign language or the finger alphabet."

"Crickets!" Pete said. "This is just what we've been looking for!"

"You mean a secret language for our club!" Pam said with enthusiasm.

"Sure!" Pete went on. "We'll be able to talk to each other without making a sound."

"We're talking with the finger alphabet."

Pam turned to Charles and said, "Will you teach us the finger alphabet?"

When the boy said yes, Pete led the way up to his room, followed by the other children and Kerry. They gave Charles a piece of white cardboard and pen and ink. He sat at the desk and began very carefully to draw pictures of a hand with the fingers in different positions, each of which meant a letter in the alphabet. Pete and Pam looked on quietly.

When Ricky began to get restless, Kerry Flip said to him and Holly and Sue, "How would you like to learn some tumbling tricks?"

They hurried down to the lawn, where Ricky said, "Show us some of your stunts first."

The acrobat did handstands, front flips, and back flips. Little Sue clapped loudest of all and cried gleefully, "You're an upside-down man!"

While Mr. and Mrs. Hollister busied themselves in the kitchen, Kerry instructed the youngsters in how to perform cart wheels. Before long, Ricky, Holly, and Sue were doing them over the lawn.

"You'd all make fine acrobats," Kerry said. "Now how would you like to build a pyramid?" The children agreed eagerly. "It's hard," he warned, "but I think we can do it."

Kerry squatted and instructed Ricky and Holly to climb on each of his shoulders.

"Steady now," he said as the children stood up and teetered. "That's right. Now hold it. Come here, Sue."

Kerry reached down and picked up the little girl.

"Now," he said, glancing left and right, "Sue will stand on your shoulders."

"Yikes!" Ricky exclaimed. "Can you hold all three of us?"

Without replying, Kerry lifted Sue high over his head and Holly and Ricky hoisted her to their shoulders. Then, slowly and smoothly, Kerry stood up, raising them all high in the air.

Even though Sue was a little frightened, she managed to giggle. But when she did she lost her balance. Her brother and sister tried to hold her upright, but the little girl swayed back and forth. Suddenly she fell forward and dropped toward the lawn far below.

CHAPTER 7

ZIP'S WARNING

KERRY FLIP stepped forward as Ricky and Holly leaped from his shoulders. He caught Sue in mid-air, twirled her around gracefully, and set her on the lawn.

"Oh, that was fun!" Sue giggled. "Let's do that again."

The acrobat thought it would be best for Ricky and Holly to practice shoulder stands longer before attempting to make another pyramid with Sue.

Ricky, especially, liked to do the trick, and he was hoisted once more to Kerry's shoulders. He balanced himself so well that the man walked about without even holding him by the ankles.

"You'd do well with a circus," the acrobat told him.

Just as their tumbling practice was over, the younger children saw Pete, Pam, and Charles emerge from the house. Their big sister held the white cardboard in her hand and waved it at them.

"We have our secret code. Come look!"

As they all crowded around, Kerry said, "Charles is very good at drawing. He made the finger alphabet perfectly."

The acrobat explained to the Hollisters that this

method of communication by the deaf was invented in Paris in the seventeenth century.

"You can speak French with this, too?" Ricky asked in amazement.

"Any language," Kerry replied with a chuckle, "so long as you know how to spell."

"This will be a project for our Detective Club," Pam said. "What fun we can have when we all learn it!"

Just then Mrs. Hollister called the children inside. "Daddy and I have packed a picnic which we will eat at the State Park," she said. "Everything is on the kitchen table for you to carry to the car."

Pete picked up a huge hamper filled with sandwiches. Charles took a large vacuum jug, and as he walked to the car with it Pam followed him, studying the finger language chart. When she spelled out *picnic*, Charles grinned and ran his tongue over his lips.

Sue sat in front with her mother and father. Kerry, Pete, Pam, and Charles squeezed into the second seat while Ricky and Holly climbed into the back. Before they had a chance to lift the tail gate, Zip, their beautiful collie, bounded into the car with them.

"Let's take him along. He'll have fun," Holly begged.

"All right," their father replied. "But we can't allow Zip to run around the picnic grounds."

"That's all right, Daddy," Sue chirped. "He can guard the car for us."

The ride to State Park was short and pleasant. The

highway carried them close to Mrs. Neeley's estate and along the lake shore for several miles.

From there they turned off into rolling countryside, and in a few minutes Mr. Hollister drove the station wagon through a gate. Beside it was a sign which read, "Shoreham State Park—Picnics and Amusements."

Even though the Hollisters had been there many times before, the thought of a cookout and riding the brightly colored merry-go-round always made them happy.

This season a carnival troupe, which included Kerry Flip, had been added to the entertainment. The performers did their act under a small tent located near the carrousel.

Mr. Hollister drove into a woodsy section and parked close to a fireplace and picnic table. "It's only a short walk from here to the amusements," he said.

After they got out, Pete rolled up the car windows nearly to the top. Zip obediently stayed inside. The girls quickly spread the table while the boys started a fire and broiled juicy hamburgers.

All during the picnic, the children took turns forming words with the finger alphabet.

When Ricky spelled out *p-i-c-k-e-l*, everybody laughed and told him he must be a better speller than that.

After a jolly meal, Kerry excused himself, saying he had to get ready for his act.

"I'll see you in a little while," he said, waving and setting off down the path toward the carnival tent.

The table was quickly cleared, the fire put out, and the picnic gear stowed in the station wagon.

"Keep an eye on things," Pete said to Zip. Then the family started off toward the entertainment center.

"I think we'll have time for a ride on the merry-go-round," Mrs. Hollister remarked, "before Kerry's show starts at four."

Pete ran ahead to purchase tickets, and soon all six children were riding up and down on the gaily marked animals of the carrousel. When it slowed down they hopped off and hurried toward the tent.

A loud-speaker announced: "Everyone is invited to see the world's greatest acrobat and tumbler—Kerry Flip and his company."

"I didn't know he owned a company, too," Ricky said.

"Those are the men he performs with," Pam told him as they bought their tickets and went through a turnstile into the many-colored tent.

They took their seats and waited. In a few minutes the buzzing conversation of the spectators ceased when Kerry Flip, dressed in red-spangled tights, came into the center of the ring. With him were four other performers.

First they tumbled and rolled, doing handstands and flips in quick succession. The onlookers clapped and cheered.

After that, trapezes and flying rings were let down from the ceiling. Kerry leaped up to grasp a trapeze bar. How gracefully he swung back and forth!!

Then he executed a double flip in mid-air, catching another swinging trapeze. As the hushed audience looked on, Pam heard Zip barking in the distance. The dog sounded frantic.

"Something must be the matter," Pam whispered to Pete as the sound was drowned out by the deafening applause.

"Excuse us, Mother," Pam said, leaning over.

When Charles saw her rise to leave with Pete, he joined them. Ricky, Holly, and Sue were so engrossed in the performance that they did not see the older children go.

The three worked their way out of the grandstand. Once outside the tent, they again heard Zip's urgent barking. Pete and Pam dashed along the woodland path, with Charles racing along behind them.

When they reached the car they could see no one, but the collie kept on yipping and yapping.

"What's the matter, old boy?" Pete asked. He opened the door halfway and the dog tried to jump out.

"No, no, it's against the rules here," Pam said. "Stay where you are, boy."

Just then Charles put his hand on Pete's shoulder, turned him around, and pointed. At the same time he said, "Man went there. I saw him."

Pete and Pam had seen nothing, but, remembering that Kerry had told them that deaf persons developed excellent side vision, they followed Charles into the brush. The branches had been broken and trampled

"Crickets! They got away!"

down. Some of them were still moving, indicating that a person had gone through shortly before.

The children followed the trail, moving quietly through the woods for several hundred yards. However, they could see no one. Finally they came to a grassy stretch which bordered Pine Lake.

"Look over there!" Pete said, pointing.

A man's head bobbed in the high grass near the lake front.

The children dashed forward. "Do you suppose he was trying to steal our picnic things?" Pam asked as they ran.

They were only halfway across the meadow when suddenly the sound of an outboard motor reached their ears.

"Oh, he's getting away!" Pete exclaimed. By the time he, Pam, and Charles reached the shore they could see a boat churning up a white wake. Its motor, painted bright yellow, was speeding it toward the center of the lake. In the craft were two men, crouching low.

Pete gazed after the motorboat until it was lost from sight.

"Crickets! They got away," Pete said soberly, and the three children retraced their steps.

By the time they had returned to the car, the performance was over and the rest of the family was waiting for them. Kerry Flip, still in his tights, said good-by. "And I hope you find that old doorway soon," he added.

On the way home, Pete asked his father to drive into Serpentine Road so that they might speak with Mrs. Neeley.

"That mystery certainly was cleared up in a hurry," Mrs. Hollister remarked as they neared the old estate.

But Pete was skeptical. His father parked beside the gate and the boy and Pam stepped out. They hastened to the gatehouse and knocked on the door. Mrs. Neeley opened it, but she was not smiling. Instead, she looked worried and a little frightened.

"I've been telephoning your house all afternoon," she told them. "Something terrible has happened."

"You mean the ghost is back?" Pete asked.

"Oh dear, yes," the woman replied. "I do hope you'll believe what I tell you. It was so frightening!"

Mrs. Neeley lowered her voice and looked over her gold-rimmed glasses to see if anyone else might be listening.

"I saw a skeleton in the sky," she said. "Right over my Antique House."

"When was this?" Pete asked.

"This morning, about four o'clock," she replied.

Mrs. Neeley said that she had heard strange moans and that, after getting up to look, she had seen the weird figure of a ghost flitting in the air directly over one of the old chimneys.

"I was too scared to talk to anybody about it," the woman said. "I didn't even want to tell you children, but I finally got up my courage and telephoned."

76

"How about Officer Cal?" Pete asked. "Did you notify him?"

"I just couldn't," Mrs. Neeley said. "The police might think I'm crazy."

Pete and Pam exchanged a quick glance. Perhaps the woman had only been dreaming.

"I know what you're thinking," the stout lady went on. "But I *did* see it!"

"We'll try to help you, Mrs. Neeley," Pam said kindly. "You'll be hearing from us." They said good-by and returned to the car.

"Did you get the reward? What was it?" Ricky asked impatiently.

The children got in and shut the door as Mr. Hollister drove away.

"There was no reward," Pete said.

"Only another spook," Pam added, and told about the skeleton in the sky.

Mr. Hollister shook his head gravely and said, "This case seems to be a mix-up of the real and the imaginary. You children might not be able to solve it."

"Oh yes, we will!" Holly said stoutly.

The conversation had been flying back and forth so rapidly that Charles did not understand what was going on. For the rest of the trip Pam wrote a note telling him about the mystery in the Antique House.

In return the boy wrote, *I'd like to join your Detective Club.*

"We can take a vote right now," Pete said. "We have enough members present. All in favor say 'aye.'"

All of the children sang out. Even Zip barked approval.

Pam turned to face the deaf boy and said, "You're a club member."

"Thank you," he replied, smiling. A few minutes later Mr. Hollister let Charles off at the farm and drove back to their home.

As the children prepared for bed, Pete spoke to Ricky. "Mr. Akers might have the prints ready tomorrow morning. Suppose you and Holly go there early." Pete added that he would assign Dave to scout around the Antique House.

"O.K., chief," the red-haired boy said, trying to imitate a real detective.

Shortly after breakfast next morning, Ricky and Holly rode their bicycles to Mr. Akers' photo shop. The man behind the counter smiled as they came in and said, "How did you like them?"

"Like what?" Ricky asked.

"The photos. Didn't you get them?"

The children looked confused.

"Didn't you send a boy in to pick up the pictures for you?" Mr. Akers asked.

"No, we didn't!" Ricky cried in alarm.

The photo shop man said that two boys had come in to ask for the pictures, saying that Ricky Hollister had sent them.

"Who were they?" Holly asked, so angry that tears came to her eyes.

Mr. Akers said that he had recognized one of them as Will Wilson.

"And I'll bet the other one was Joey Brill!" Ricky said, his eyes flashing.

"It could have been," Mr. Akers replied. "They took the pictures and charged them to you."

CHAPTER 8

A MUD BATH

UNABLE to hold back her tears any longer, Holly started to cry. Losing the prints was bad enough, but now Kerry Flip's original photograph was gone, too. What would the acrobat think of their detective work? His mystery might never be solved.

Ricky put an arm around his sister and offered her his handkerchief. "Come on, we can't waste any time," he said. "We'll go to Joey Brill's house right away and get those pictures!"

It did not take them long to reach Joey's house. After parking their bicycles, they walked up to the front door and rang the bell beside the screen door.

Mrs. Brill answered it. Seeing the children, she raised her eyebrows and said, "Yes? What do you want?"

Holly's eyes were still red from her weeping. Her chin quivered as she spoke up. "Joey got our pictures at the photo shop. We want them back!"

"I'm sure there must be some mistake," Mrs. Brill said. "Why would he want pictures of you?"

"They were not of us," Ricky hastened to explain. He told the woman about Kerry Flip's precious clue and how they hoped to solve his mystery.

"Joey is not interested in your Detective Club," the woman went on. "He would have no reason to take those pictures."

"But he did!" Ricky insisted. "Mr. Akers recognized Will Wilson for sure."

Mrs. Brill looked down at them for a moment. She went inside the house and returned with her son. Joey's hands were thrust in his pockets and his head was lowered.

"Do you have the Hollisters' pictures?" his mother asked.

"No."

"Does Will Wilson have them?"

"No."

"How can you be so mean, Joey Brill!" Holly said, and began to sob. Ricky handed her his handkerchief again.

Joey's mother felt sorry for the little girl. She tilted her son's chin up so that his eyes looked directly into hers. "Joey, do you know anything about those pictures?" Her voice was stern. "Tell me the truth."

Joey flinched and scowled uncomfortably at Ricky and Holly.

"All right!" he declared. "If these kids can't take a joke, it's not my fault."

"It doesn't seem to be funny to Holly," his mother snapped. "Where are those pictures?"

"I don't have 'em any more," Joey said.

"Well, where are they?" Ricky spoke up.

"We got rid of 'em."

"Where?" his mother prompted the boy.

"Down by the lake front."

Mrs. Brill sighed. "I get so tired of having trouble between you and the Hollisters," she told her son tartly. "You had no business taking their pictures. Now come and show me where they are."

Even though the lake front was two blocks from where Joey lived, his mother marched him off in that direction with a determined step. Ricky and Holly followed close behind.

When they reached the shore, the waves were lapping gently over pebbles and rocks on the stony beach. Joey looked more embarrassed than ever as he pointed. "The pictures are over there."

"I can't see them," his mother said.

"They're under that rock!"

He pointed to a large flat stone which lay half in, half out of the water.

"Oh dear!" Holly cried. "They'll be all wet!"

Ricky tiptoed over the muddy shore and dug his fingers under the edge of the stone and lifted it. Underneath lay the package of pictures. It was soaked through with mud and water.

"They're ruined!" Ricky said, and showed the soiled and soggy pictures to Mrs. Brill.

"I'm sorry," she said. "Please tell your——" Mrs. Brill glanced about to scold her son. But he had raced off toward a thicket near the water front. "Joey, come back here!" his mother called. But the boy did not heed her.

"Wait till your father comes home tonight," Mrs.

"Hey, cut it out!" the bully cried.

Brill called out, and set off after him. When she could not find him, she continued on to her house.

Ricky and Holly looked at each other in dismay.

"What will we do now?" Ricky said. "The pictures are all spoiled."

"We might just as well have lost them," Holly said. "Even the old photo that Kerry Flip gave us is a mess."

Just then there was a shout nearby and Joey raced from his hiding place in the thicket.

"I'll get you for squealing on me!" he declared as he rushed toward the two children. Ricky slipped the pictures into his pocket, and none too soon. Joey sprang upon the brother and sister, throwing them into the mud.

"Oh!" Holly cried, struggling to her feet. "Oh, you—you——"

With fire in her eyes and her muddy pigtails flying, Holly leaped at Joey Brill. At the same time Ricky struggled out of the goo and grasped Joey by the ankles.

"Hey, cut it out!" the bully cried. Off balance, he fell into the mud, and all three rolled over and over in the struggle.

As Joey bellowed, Ricky scooped up a handful of mud and plastered it on his face.

"Oh-uh glug."

In the seconds that followed, all three children were turned into brown, slippery blobs.

Still spluttering, Joey pulled himself away from the other two and dashed toward his house.

Ricky and Holly walked dejectedly along the shore line until they reached their own home. Pete and Pam had carried one of the newly painted chairs onto the dock. Mrs. Hollister was seated in it, enjoying the morning sunshine. White Nose was in her lap. Pete and Pam were sitting at her feet practicing the finger alphabet.

As crestfallen Ricky and Holly walked over to them, the group could hardly believe their eyes.

"What happened to you!" their mother cried out.

When White Nose saw the two muddy children, she meowed, jumped out of Mrs. Hollister's lap, and raced up a willow tree.

"Even the cat doesn't know you," Pam said. "You're a fright!"

Ricky and his sister told what had happened to them.

"Anyhow," Holly said, "Joey's just as gooky as we are."

Ricky pulled the pictures from his pocket and handed them to Pete.

"First thing you do is to jump in the lake," their mother said, "and get rid of some of that mud."

The two children immediately brightened. Ricky often had wanted to jump into the lake with his clothes on. Now he had a chance. Holding Holly by the hand, he leaped off the edge of the dock and swam about gleefully, shedding the mud from his clothes, face, and hair. When they climbed out of the water they were dripping wet but reasonably clean.

"Now into the house for a good shower," their mother said, "and then some lunch."

She took personal charge of scrubbing Holly. Her hair had to be dried and her pigtails braided again.

When the girl was freshly dressed in clean shorts, shirt, and dry shoes, she ran down to the dining room, where Ricky was talking with Pete and Pam.

"I know we're awful detectives," Holly said. "What will Kerry Flip say when he hears his pictures are ruined?"

"We can fix that all right," Pete told her.

"How?" Ricky questioned.

The older boy explained that Mr. Akers had had to take a photo of the old picture. Then, from one negative of it, he had made the eight new prints.

"I found that negative in the package," Pete said, "and now we can have more pictures made. While you were taking showers I cleaned and dried it." He showed it to them. "It's as good as new. You can take it to Mr. Akers after we eat."

"But then we'll have to wait a couple of days for the prints," Ricky said. "Let's take it to Mr. Fundy. He said he'd do a favor for us. Maybe he can make some right away."

Pete and Pam agreed that this was a good idea.

After lunch Ricky and Holly set off for the second time. They found Mr. Fundy at home, and he said he would be glad to help them.

The white-haired man held the negative up to the light. "This is a good one," he said. "I could even make an enlargement. Would you like to watch me do it?"

Ricky and Holly no longer had glum faces. Their rosy cheeks glowed as they smiled at Mr. Fundy. He took them into his darkroom, inserted the negative into an enlarger, and turned off the room light.

Mr. Fundy flicked a switch. A dim glow shone from the enlarger onto a piece of sensitized paper. The light clicked off again and he put the paper into a tray of developing fluid. As if by magic, the pictures of the little girl appeared.

"Oh, goody!" Holly cried out in delight as Ricky whistled between his teeth.

The old photographer made eight prints, which he developed and washed in running water. Then he said, "Now I'll make the bigger one." A few minutes later a large photo of Kerry's mother appeared in the tray of developer.

"Oh," Holly said. "Mr. Flip will love this."

When all the pictures had been dried, the youngsters thanked the old man and hastily pedaled back home again.

"Look what we have!" Ricky cried as they raced into the house with the photographs.

Pete, Pam, and Mrs. Hollister were amazed to see the enlargement. Pam looked at it carefully.

Suddenly she hurried to get a magnifying glass, which her mother kept in the desk.

"Ricky! Holly! Look!!" Pam cried as she peered through it. "You've discovered a great clue!"

CHAPTER 9

A MIX-UP

"LOOK HERE," Pam said, pointing at the enlarged photograph. The stone step, on which the little girl was standing, bore the faint numerals 1803.

"Crickets!" Pete cried out. "It's lucky you had this made bigger. Otherwise we wouldn't have been able to see that old date."

"That must have been the year the house was built," Pam reasoned. "All we have to do is find the places put up that year and we can locate the one Kerry Flip is looking for."

The Hollisters discussed how this could best be done. Pam suggested visiting the local library to look through books about the early days in Shoreham. Pete thought the newspaper office might have a clipping of a story about old houses which might help them.

Their discussion was interrupted by the ringing of the telephone. Pete answered it.

"Hello, Dave," he said. "Anything new at the Antique House?" He listened for a moment, his eyes keen with interest.

When he hung up, Holly said, "What's the latest?"

Pete told them that Dave reported there were no

visitors in the Antique House. It would be a good time for another search of the premises.

"I know what," Ricky said. "Pete, why don't you and I scout around there with Dave while the girls go to the library?"

"Good idea," Pam said; "only I can't go."

"Why?" Holly asked.

"I promised Mother that I would tidy the pantry today." She looked wistful and added, "I don't like to give up my sleuthing with such a good clue to work on."

Without hesitation Holly spoke up. "I'll stay home and clean the pantry. Sue can help me, and maybe Donna Martin, too."

Pam hugged her pig-tailed sister. "Oh, thank you, honey! You're sweet to do that."

As she hurried to phone Ann Hunter to meet her at the library, the boys started for the yard to get their bicycles. At the front door Ricky paused. "Full steam ahead on both mysteries, men!" he commanded, saluted, and was gone.

A few minutes later Pam was ready to leave. "Now don't forget to wash everything," she told her younger sister.

After Pam had gone, Holly woke Sue from her nap and they skipped down the street to where Donna Martin lived. The plump child was sitting on her porch steps.

"Did you come over to play with my dollhouse?" Donna smiled, showing her dimples.

Holly giggled and replied, "We're going to play

real house today. Why don't you come down?" She explained the plan.

"Oh, I just love to clean pantries," Donna said. The two girls held hands and ran across the lawn towards the Hollister house.

The pantry was a large walk-in closet entered by a door in the kitchen. It was bright and cheerful, having a window high on the outside wall.

Shelf after shelf was covered with red and white paper, and on them were stacked neat rows of canned goods, spices, bottles of ketchup, maple sugar, and other good things to eat. On the bottom one stood yellow canisters of flour and sugar.

"This will be fun to clean," Donna said as the three girls surveyed their chore.

"And Mother wants everything washed," Holly reminded her friend.

First the playmates went into the basement, where they got two buckets and half-filled them with warm water. They added a little detergent to each. The older girls carried the pails upstairs and Sue followed with a handful of soft cloths. Holly suggested that everything be taken from the pantry shelves and placed on the kitchen table.

"I think that's the way Mother does it," she said.

"Where is your mother?" Donna asked.

Sue replied that Mrs. Hollister had gone downtown shopping and would not return home until later in the afternoon.

"Won't Mother be surprised!" Holly said as she

and Donna got a small folding stepladder from the broom closet and set it up in the pantry.

"I'll get the things from the top shelf and hand them to you, Donna," Holly said. "Then you can give them to Sue and she'll put them on the table."

Working like a bucket brigade used by firemen in olden times, the three girls cleared the pantry shelves. Now the kitchen table, stacked high with cans and bottles, resembled the sky line of a large city.

It was agreed that Sue should clean the canned goods while Holly and her friend wiped the shelves of the pantry. The two older girls took their buckets inside and closed the door, leaving little Sue alone with her job.

The child put her finger in her mouth and thought for a moment. Then she pulled a chair up to the kitchen sink and turned on the warm-water faucet.

"Hmm, that's about right," the little girl said to herself when the sink was half full.

She climbed down from the chair, went to the table, and gathered an armful of canned goods. One by one she carefully dropped them into the warm water.

Soon the kitchen sink was full of cans. They were piled nearly as high as the faucet. Then, in order to do a thorough cleaning job, Sue took the rubber hose spray and drenched them all thoroughly.

"Mommy will like this," the little girl told herself as she started to lift the clean cans back to the table. But, as she did, the labels slipped off into the water. "Goodness," Sue said aloud. Then she dried each unlabeled can carefully and set it back on the table.

By this time Holly and Donna had finished their task and opened the pantry door. When Holly saw the bare cans, her eyes grew wide and her lips parted in surprise.

"Sue, what have you done!" she exclaimed, running over to look at the table and then glancing into the kitchen sink, where the labels floated gently in the warm water.

"Mother said to wash everything, didn't she?" Sue asked. "So I did."

"But the labels!" Donna said, aghast. "The labels aren't on the cans any more."

"Oh, we can fix that all right," Sue said. "I have some paste in my room. "I'll get it."

She hurried off, and Holly and Donna looked at each other in shocked dismay. Quickly they removed the labels from the sink and dried them between kitchen towels.

When Sue returned with the paste the girls carefully replaced the labels on the cans. Then they began putting things back on the shelves.

As Holly replaced the last can, she glanced out the pantry window and said, "Here come Pam and Ann. I wonder what they discovered in the library."

"Hello. Are the boys back yet?" Pam called out as she and her friend hurried into the kitchen.

"Not yet," Holly answered. She added, "See what we did!"

The two older girls looked into the pantry. It was spick and span.

"What a grand job!" Pam remarked. "Mother will appreciate this." She and Ann walked in to admire the clean shelves.

"I helped, too," Sue piped up. "I——"

Holly grabbed Sue by the hand and whisked her out the back door, followed by Donna.

"Sh-sh, let's not tell Pam about the labels yet," Holly said, looking nervously about.

"Maybe later," Donna added in a low voice. The little girl agreed to keep the secret. At least for a while.

Pam and Ann joined them in the yard.

"Oh, I wish the boys were here," Pam said. "I have something to tell them."

Pete, Ricky, and Dave, meanwhile, had met at the gatehouse.

"I have some questions to ask you about that skeleton in the sky, Mrs. Neeley," Pete said. "You told us you saw this at four o'clock in the morning. What was the weather like?"

"I don't see what that has to do with it," the stout woman replied. Then she thought for a moment. "It was very dark. I could not see the moon or stars. In fact, the clouds were very low."

Pete noted these facts in a small notebook which he carried.

"Thanks," he said. He added, "Do you mind if we look around the place again, Mrs. Neeley?"

"No. This is a good time, since no customers are browsing about," she replied.

The boys hastened to the Antique House, quietly opened the front door, and stepped inside. Everything was silent.

"Let's go up to the third floor," Pete suggested. "We haven't looked around there yet."

The companions tiptoed upstairs. When they reached the second-floor balcony Dave suddenly stopped.

"What's that?" he said, listening intently.

From the floor above them came an eerie creaking sound. Taking the stairway to their right, the boys moved slowly without making a sound. At the top they found themselves in a narrow corridor. The creaking continued, then ended with a thud.

Dave, leading the way, dashed into a small room off the hall, from which the noise had come. Chills danced up and down his spine as he looked about. It was empty except for a huge chest on one wall near a dormer window and a small oval braided rug on the floor.

Pete went close to his brother and whispered in his ear, "That's the window where we saw the light."

"Are you sure?"

Pete nodded. "I think so."

The three boys conferred in whispers. Then they hunkered down and rolled the rug to one side of the room. The wide old floor boards showed no sign of a trap door or any other secret compartment.

"There's nothing here that could creak," Pete murmured as they replaced the rug.

"How did it fall?"

"How about the walls?" Ricky asked. "Maybe some of them are hollow."

The three boys began tapping the sides of the room when suddenly *crash!* The sound of shattering glass came from the second floor.

They raced into the hall and leaped down the steps. On the second-floor balcony they found a broken lamp lying on the floor beside a small drop-leaf table, which stood next to a round window.

"How did it fall?" Ricky asked with a frightened look at Pete and Dave. "There's nobody in here but us—is there?"

"There must be some explanation," Pete said. He recalled that once a glass pitcher had fallen off a shelf at The Trading Post because of the vibrations caused by heavy traffic passing the store.

"But there are no vibrations out here," Dave reminded him. "Trucks come nowhere near this place."

Pete carefully examined the table and then shook his head. "This is a real mystery," he declared, his gaze wandering through the round window to the sparkling waters of Pine Lake. Suddenly he exclaimed, "Look, the yellow outboard motor!"

The boys pressed their faces to the pane. Not far offshore was a boat which looked very much like the one in which the two men had made their getaway at the State Park. This time only one man was in the boat. He sat at the tiller, his shoulders crouched against the breeze.

"I'd like to get a better look at that fellow," Pete said. "Come on!"

Leaving the broken lamp on the floor, the trio ran downstairs, out of the door, and toward the lake shore. The man in the boat glanced their way. Seeing them, he hunched lower and sped away.

"He sure wants to keep away from us," Pete said as the boat disappeared around a point of land.

"Shall we chase along the shore and try to follow him?" Dave asked.

"He's too far ahead," his friend replied. "Anyway, we'd better tell Mrs. Neeley about the broken lamp," Pete said, "and pick up the pieces for her."

On the way back to the gatehouse the boys pondered the mysterious motorboat and its driver.

"Do you suppose he could have come from across the lake?" Dave asked.

Pete turned to gaze over the broad expanse of water. "Maybe he came from Stony Point." This was a town located on the opposite shore of Pine Lake.

A few minutes later they knocked on the gatehouse door.

Upon hearing about the broken lamp, Mrs. Neeley rubbed her chubby hands together and said, "Oh dear, one of my best antiques. Are you sure you boys didn't knock it over?"

"Honest," Ricky said, and the boys told exactly what had happened.

"The ghost again?" the woman said in a mournful voice.

"Don't worry." Pete tried to comfort her. "We're doing all we can, Mrs. Neeley. Be patient. We'll solve this case."

After the boys had swept up the broken pieces of the lamp and given them to her, they returned to their homes. Pete and Ricky found that supper was nearly ready.

"Wash your hands and come to the table," Mrs. Hollister told them.

"Where's Pam?" Pete asked.

"She walked Ann Hunter home," came the reply. "She'll be here any moment."

When the whole family was seated at the supper table, Mr. Hollister said, "What have my detectives been doing today?"

"Tell us what happened at the Antique House first," Pam said, and her brothers related the strange happenings of the afternoon.

"I have a hunch that man in the boat might be linked up to the ghost in the mansion," Pete said. "We're going to keep our eyes open for that yellow outboard. How did you make out, Pam?"

His sister told them that she and Ann had not met with much luck. "The library had no books on houses built before the Civil War," she said, "so Ann and I went to the newspaper office."

"No luck there either?" Ricky asked as he lifted his glass of milk.

Pam shook her head. "There were no clippings about ancient houses," she said, "but the editor told me about a possible clue."

"What was that?" Mr. Hollister inquired, showing great interest in his children's activities.

Pam replied that there was a retired architect,

named Mr. Drew Shaffer, who lived at Stony Point.

"Old houses are his hobby," Pam said. "The editor suggested that we visit him. Perhaps he might know something about pre-Civil War homes in the Shoreham area."

"I've heard of Mr. Shaffer," her father put in. "A fine gentleman. He'll probably be glad to help you if he can."

Then Pam told her mother about how Holly, Sue, and Donna had taken over her pantry chore.

"It looks lovely and sparkling clean," Mrs. Hollister said, smiling at her daughters.

"What's for dessert, Mom?" Ricky asked.

"How would you like cherries?" Mrs. Hollister asked. "There's a can in the pantry."

Holly gulped and looked down at her plate while Ricky spouted, "Yikes, I like cherries."

"I'll open a can for you, Elaine," the children's father said, rising from his chair.

He went to the pantry. The children could hear the faint sound of the can opener. Holly closed her eyes tight and wished hard.

Suddenly Mr. Hollister's voice boomed from the kitchen. "Great horned toads! What kind of cherries are these!"

CHAPTER 10

OFFICER CAL'S SURPRISE

"ELAINE," Mr. Hollister said to his wife as he entered the dining room, carrying an opened can in his hand, "when did cherries change to onions!"

His wife gasped in surprise. The can, labeled cherries, was filled with tiny white onions.

"Goodness, I'll have to tell the grocer about this," she declared. Holly and Sue exchanged sidewise glances but said nothing.

"Open a can of pears, John," Mrs. Hollister went on. "Everybody likes pears."

Her husband set the can of onions on the pantry shelf, selected another can marked pears, and opened it. His cry of disbelief startled the rest of the family. This time Mrs. Hollister rose from her chair and hurried to see what was the matter. The children followed her.

"Beans!" their father burst out. "What's going on here, Elaine?"

"Maybe the grocer's trying to play tricks on us," Pete remarked.

"Well, I'll find out this minute," Mrs. Hollister declared, and reached for the wall telephone.

"Wait, Mommy," Holly said. "It's my fault!"

Her mother returned the receiver to the telephone and looked down at her daughter with a quizzical expression. "How could it be your fault?"

Suddenly little Sue flung her arms around her mother, buried her head in her skirt, and began to cry. She wept so that her shoulders shook.

"Gracious, why all the tears?" her mother asked, picking up the little girl and holding her in her arms.

"The labels came off!" Sue blurted between sobs.

"Yes, and I helped paste them back on the wrong cans," Holly added. "I'm so sorry, Mother."

Soon the entire story was out.

"Yikes, what a mistake!" Ricky remarked, and Pam gave him a stern look.

"Don't worry, either of you," their mother said. She hugged Sue and Holly and praised them for being helpful to their big sister.

By this time a smile had crept over Mr. Hollister's lips. "Another big mystery to solve. Let's call this the case of the missing dessert."

All the children laughed. Even Sue's wet cheeks dimpled.

"Hmm," Mr. Hollister said, "I wonder what to open next."

"Try the spinach," Ricky said, joking.

Mr. Hollister reached for it. Even before his wife could protest, he put the can in the opener. *Zing*. The lid was off. Inside, pink and white cherries floated around in the syrup.

"Hurray for Daddy!" Holly exclaimed, clapping and jumping up and down. "He solved the mystery!"

"But what about all the other cans?" Mrs. Hollister asked, rolling her eyes and pouring the fruit in a large bowl. She quickly added with a chuckle, "Guess we'll have to take potluck until we use them all."

Everybody started to laugh, and the giggling lasted until the supper dishes were washed and put away.

"What an exciting day!" Pam exclaimed as she prepared for bed.

Just then Holly poked her head in Pam's room. "Maybe tomorrow nothing at all will happen," she said.

The next morning was bright and sunny. Breakfast went by quietly, and it seemed as if Holly's prediction might come true—until the mailman arrived.

Pam took the handful of letters from the postman and hurried into the house. Riffling through the letters, she was hoping there would be one from their cousin. But the mail was mostly advertisements and a few bills.

Then her eyes came to rest on a most unusual envelope. It was addressed to "The Hollisters," and each of the letters had been cut from a newspaper and glued onto it.

Pam called Pete, then her mother. After she had shown them the letter, she said, "Perhaps you had better open it, Mother, because it's addressed to the family."

Pete went for a letter opener and handed it to his mother. She slit the envelope and pulled out a piece of white paper. It, too, had cutout letters glued on it. The message said:

WARNING. STAY AWAY FROM THE ANTIQUE HOUSE.

"Oh dear!" Mrs. Hollister murmured. "This is terrible."

"Maybe it's a joke," Pete said. "It could be from Joey Brill."

But Pam did not agree. "I don't think he's smart enough to think of this method," she objected. "Joey would probably just scribble a note."

"Pam's right," her mother said. "Whoever sent this wants to make sure that nobody recognizes his handwriting."

"I'd better phone Officer Cal right away," Pete said, reaching for the telephone on the desk.

Headquarters, however, informed him that their friend was out of town on another case and would not be back for the rest of the day.

After Pete told the others, he said, "The Detective Club ought not to go to the Antique House any more until Officer Cal hears about this note. We're stuck for a while," he added, frowning.

"Why don't we all work on Kerry Flip's mystery today?" Pam suggested. "We could go to Stony Point to see Mr. Shaffer, the architect."

Mrs. Hollister said that she had a friend who lived at Stony Point. "Let's all go there for an outing. Sue

Mrs. Hollister read the warning note.

and I will visit Mrs. Dillon while the rest of you children talk with Mr. Shaffer."

Pete and Pam were delighted at their mother's suggestion, and Pam volunteered to tell her other brother and sisters. Meanwhile, Pete telephoned the club members to advise them about the note.

Half an hour later all six were in the station wagon. Mrs. Hollister smiled at the enthusiasm of her young detectives as she drove along a beautiful highway bordering Pine Lake.

At noontime, when they reached the outskirts of Stony Point, Mrs. Hollister stopped at a roadside refreshment stand. There everyone had sandwiches, milk, and ice cream.

Minutes later they were in the quaint little town of Stony Point. Pam asked a policeman for directions to Mr. Shaffer's place, and soon the Hollisters found themselves in front of a neat modern house.

"It's a beauty!" Pete said.

"You can see that a good architect designed it," Mrs. Hollister remarked. "I'll be back for you in an hour," she added as Pete, Pam, Ricky, and Holly stepped out of the car.

When their mother saw a man reply to their knock on the door and ask them in, she drove off with Sue.

Pam liked Mr. Shaffer the moment she saw him. He was small and slightly stooped, with thin sandy hair and a little goatee.

"I'm delighted to have callers," the man said. "Step right in, children. Do the girls want me to design a dollhouse for them?"

"No," Holly replied. "We're detectives and we're looking for clues."

Pam made the introductions and each child shook hands with Mr. Shaffer. Then he ushered them into the living room. "I'll try to help you if I can," he said. "Sit down and tell me all about it."

The architect listened quietly, occasionally tugging at his goatee, while Pete and Pam told their story.

When they had finished, Pete reached into his pocket and pulled out a copy of Kerry Flip's picture. "This is the doorway we're looking for, Mr. Shaffer. Have you ever seen one like it?"

The man took the photograph and examined it closely. "No, I haven't," he said finally. Then he mumbled, "Too bad. Too bad."

"What's too bad, Mr. Shaffer?" Holly asked.

The architect replied that several months before he had purchased a collection of plans of pre-Civil War houses in the area. "But I didn't have time to read them carefully," he said. "They were stolen from my den along with some valuable gems."

"Crickets!" Pete declared. "Did you say gems?"

"That's right," came the reply. "I think that my family jewels were the thief's main interest. But he also took the sketches of the old houses, which would have been of great value to you children."

"Did your local police find any leads?" Pam asked.

"Not a thing. The culprit made a clean getaway."

"I think we know the man who can help you,"

Pete said. "Officer Cal of our town is investigating gem thefts which have taken place in this area."

"He's a very good policeman," Holly put in. "His name is——"

Mr. Shaffer held up his hand. "Wait," he said. He walked into the next room and returned a few moments later. With him was a handsome young man dressed in a gray suit.

A few seconds later, when the Hollisters realized who it was, they stared in astonishment.

CHAPTER 11

THE GLUE CLUE

"Yikes!" Ricky cried out. "Officer Cal!"

"We didn't know you in civilian clothes!" Pete exclaimed.

Pam smiled, delighted to see their friend.

Cal Newberry laughed as Holly ran forward and threw her arms around him.

When they were all seated, the policeman said: "You know that I've been investigating gem thefts in and around Shoreham, but this trip is secret. I don't want you to mention that you saw me here."

"Oh, we won't," Pam promised. "Have you found out anything?"

Officer Cal said that bits of information he had picked up at the scenes of the robberies had led him to think that the thieves had come to Stony Point.

"The culprits have a hide-out somewhere around here," he said, "and I am trying to find it."

Pete thought immediately about the two men in the motorboat and told Officer Cal about this. When the officer jotted it down, Pete went on to report the threatening note that the family had received.

The policeman frowned. "That could be the work of a crank or the real thing," he said. "Bring the note to headquarters. We'll see if we can trace it. And from now on you children be very careful."

Pam then asked Mr. Shaffer if he could recall something about the old houses in Shoreham.

"Yes," he said. "Even though I didn't have time to examine the sketches carefully, I remember that there were three houses in your town built in the early 1800s.

"One of them," he continued, "is the Keene homestead. This is a Cape Cod type house surrounded by big fields. The present owners keep horses. The second's known as the Adams' Castle because of its stone turrets.

"And the third place," he concluded, "is the old Miller mansion. It's known as the Antique House now."

"We've looked all around it," Pam said, "but there is no door like the one on Kerry Flip's photo."

"Thanks very much," Pete told Mr. Shaffer. "We'll investigate those other two places right away."

Shortly afterward the children heard the horn of their car outside and they said good-by.

"You can tell your parents you saw me here," Officer Cal told them, "but no one else."

Holly put her finger to her lips and said, "We'll keep your secret." Then she hugged the policeman, and the children left.

"Well, what did you find out?" their mother asked as they piled into the station wagon.

Pam told her of the two new places that they would

investigate. Mrs. Hollister knew where the Keene homestead and Adams' Castle were. Both were located in the oldest section of town, adjacent to lovely rolling woodland.

Mrs. Hollister started the car and drove along the shore road which led to the main highway. The family arrived home late in the afternoon. After supper, Pete and Pam asked permission to visit the old houses that Mr. Shaffer had mentioned.

When Mrs. Hollister said yes, it was decided that Pam and Ricky should go to the Keene homestead. Pete and Holly would visit Adams' Castle. It was a medium-long bicycle ride to both places, and the children promised to be home before dusk.

The four pedaled down the road a little way, then separated. Pam and Ricky took the road to the Keene homestead.

They found it to be a beautiful white house set far back from the highway. The lane leading to it was lined on either side by tall poplar trees.

"I think we'd better ask the people if we can look around," Pam said as she fingered the photo in her dress pocket.

The children stood their bicycles against a tree and rang the doorbell. No one answered.

"Nobody's home," Ricky said.

Pam led the way around the side of the house. To the rear was a large barn, and behind it a meadow which stretched to the edge of the woods.

"I see a man way over there." Ricky pointed into the fields.

"Whoa!" Pam commanded.

As they trudged past the barn, the children glanced back at the house, but there was no doorway like the one in the photograph. Halfway across the grassy stretch, Pam and Ricky were suddenly startled by hoofbeats behind them. They turned to see a horse galloping straight toward them. They started to run. "Help!" Ricky screamed.

Now the great animal was nearly upon them. Pam whirled about, held her hands high in the air, and cried, "Whoa!"

The horse reared to a halt inches from her.

Meanwhile, the man in the field had run up. "Hold it, Champ!" he commanded. Then he asked the children who they were.

When Pam told him, he introduced himself as Mr. Fuller, the caretaker of the property. "A mean boy once hit Champ," he told them, "and he's been unfriendly to youngsters ever since."

"That's too bad," Pam remarked, and stroked the horse's nose.

"But he seems to like you all right," Mr. Fuller observed with a chuckle. "Perhaps he won't chase children any more now."

Ricky said he hoped not, then showed the man the picture of the old doorway. "We thought perhaps it might be the Keene homestead," he explained.

The caretaker shook his head. He led Pam and Ricky back to the house and showed them all the doorways there. None matched Kerry Flip's picture.

After thanking Mr. Fuller, the brother and sister

mounted their bicycles and set off for home. Half-way there they met Pete and Holly.

"Any luck?" the older boy called out.

"None," Ricky said. "How about you?"

"Ours was a goose chase, too," Pete replied.

It was almost dark when they reached home. Their mother met them at the door. "Did you see Charles Belden?" she asked.

"No," Pete answered. "Was he here?"

The mother said that the deaf boy had stopped by and had seemed very excited. "He had some Detective Club news for you," she said, "and promised to come back in the morning."

Since it was too late for them to go to see their friend, they practiced the finger alphabet until bed-time.

At nine o'clock the next morning Mr. Johnson, the farmer, pulled up in front of the Hollister home with Charles.

The boy hurried to the porch, where the children were sitting on the steps, waiting for him. He tried forming his words but was too excited. Instead, he spelled the message with his fingers.

Charles reported that at about five o'clock the evening before he had been fishing on the lake and had seen two men walking on the shore near the Antique House. After beaching his boat, he had followed the strangers. They had paused for a moment, then suddenly had disappeared in the heavy brush. At the place where he had seen them standing Charles had found an empty tube of glue.

He held it out for Pam to see.

"Is this some kind of clue?" Ricky asked slowly. Charles read his lips and, forming his words carefully, replied, "Warning note."

"I get it!" Pete exclaimed. "He thinks these men may have pasted the letters on it with the glue from this tube."

The deaf boy nodded his head and smiled.

"Holly, will you get the note, please?" Pam said. "It's on the desk in my room."

The girl's pigtails stood straight out as she raced to do the errand. When she returned with the paper the children examined it closely.

Pam sniffed the glue around the edges of the letters, then the curled-up tube.

"They smell alike," she remarked.

"I'll taste them," Holly said impishly. Her tongue flicked out against the spent tube of glue and the mucilage on the warning note.

"They're the same!" she announced. "They taste just alike."

Pete chuckled. "Real scientific investigation by our Detective Club," he declared, and the others laughed.

"I have to go," Charles said, and pointed to the farmer, whose truck was waiting. But before the boy departed, Pete arranged to meet him that evening near the place where he had seen the two men.

During the afternoon, Pam telephoned Kerry Flip. She told him about their visits to Mr. Shaffer and the two old houses.

"Thank you, Pam," the acrobat said. "My troupe

has only a few days more at the State Park. Then I'll move on. It looks as if my mystery won't be solved."

Pam urged Kerry not to give up hope. "We'll keep on trying to help you," she promised.

After hanging up, Pam thought hard about what further action they might take in order to locate the old doorway. But for the moment she was stumped and ruefully admitted to herself that this was one mystery that she might not be able to clear up.

Near dusk, Pete set off on foot to meet Charles on the shore near the Antique House. As he approached the appointed spot, the sun went down and heavy clouds rolled in over the lake. The water looked leaden and gloomy as it lapped on the shore.

Pete spied his friend, who was sitting behind a large boulder waiting for him.

"I saw them again," Charles said with his finger alphabet.

"Where are they now?"

"They vanished!"

The boy led Pete to where he had seen the men. Their footprints were plainly visible in the soft earth. But the clouds were settling even lower, and it grew suddenly dark, making further search impossible.

Pete motioned to Charles that they would head for the Antique House. Perhaps the men were prowling around there this very moment.

As the boys approached the old mansion the wind whipped through the trees, making a weird whistling sound. Suddenly Charles grabbed Pete's arm and uttered a cry of alarm. Pete followed the boy's gaze and gasped.

A skeleton was drifting in the clouds above the Antique House!

CHAPTER 12

A LOOKOUT

To PETE's surprise the skeleton appeared for a moment among the gray clouds, then vanished.

Charles tugged at his sleeve. His eyes were wide as he asked, "What is it?"

Pete faced his deaf friend and spoke carefully, "It's some kind of a stunt. But I'm glad we saw it."

"Why?"

"Because it proves that Mrs. Neeley is no crackpot. She has been reporting the truth."

Charles nodded to show he had understood.

Pete beckoned him to follow, and the two boys walked stealthily around the house several times. Neither of them saw anything to arouse his suspicions, and Pete heard nothing.

Next they went to the gatehouse. Mrs. Neeley was happy to see them and did not mention the ghost in the sky. The Hollister boy was glad she had not seen it again.

As he and Charles started home, Pete touched his friend's arm to get his attention and said, "I think someone's trying to scare the wits out of Mrs. Neeley. It may be for a joke or for something much more serious."

Charles looked thoughtful. "Maybe," he said haltingly, "two men."

"Maybe," Pete agreed. "We're going to have to get a better look at those fellows."

"How?"

Pete stopped walking and scanned the lake shore, thinking. Suddenly he pointed to an oak which towered above the brush not far from the spot where the two men had been seen.

"We can build a tree house and spy on those men through binoculars," he said excitedly.

Charles nodded eagerly.

"Everybody in our Detective Club can help," Pete continued. "We'll start tomorrow." He told Charles that he would get in touch with him, and the two boys parted and hurried home.

First thing next morning Pete organized his work crew. By nine o'clock Jeff and Ann Hunter, as well as Dave Mead, were at the Hollister home. Ricky was busy pulling short lengths of board from an overhead rack in the garage while Holly piled the wood alongside the driveway. Donna Martin, dressed in dungarees, came and helped them.

Pete emerged from the back door carrying a hammer, a saw, a coil of rope, and a small bucket of nails.

"Indy should be here any minute with the truck," he called out to Dave.

Indy, who was named Edward Roades and was a real Indian from the West, worked at The Trading Post. Pete's father had agreed to let Indy drive the tree house work crew and their material to the oak. Mr. Hollister's truck had stake sides so that the children could ride in the back without danger of falling out.

"Here he comes now!" Ricky cried out from his perch on the ladder.

Indy sounded the horn several times, stopped the truck, and stepped out. He was a short stocky man with jet-black hair and a smile which showed his even, white teeth.

"Everybody ready?" he asked. He walked to the pile of boards. Dave and Pete helped him load them and the tools onto the back of the truck.

"There's more lumber waiting for us at Dave's place and at the Hunters' house," Pete said. "We'll pick them up on the way."

Pam and Ann sat on the front seat with Indy. Dave, Pete, Ricky, Jeff, Donna, and Holly climbed into the back.

Just as the truck was about to set off, Sue raced from the house, followed by her mother. Mrs. Hollister carried a picnic basket in her left hand and waved with her right.

"Don't forget your lunch," she called out. Ann Hunter opened the door and the mother set the picnic hamper at her feet.

"I wish I could go with you," Sue said, rocking on her heels, "but Mommy has to fit my new dress."

"You can see the tree house when we finish it, honey," Pam told her.

Then the truck set off.

Two stops were made and more boards thrown onto the back of the truck.

"That's a good supply now," Pete remarked as they started again.

Indy Roades drove along Serpentine Road for a short distance. Then he turned left into a narrow lane which led to the shore.

"This is as far as I can go," he said as he stopped the truck. All the children jumped out.

"There's the tree over there," Pete told them, pointing a hundred yards down the shore.

"That's good and high and has plenty of branches," Ricky said. Indy helped the youngsters carry the lumber and tools to a grassy spot beneath the big oak.

"When shall I call for you?" he asked.

Pete put his hands on his hips, looked the tree up and down, eyed the pile of lumber, and said, "We should have her finished by three o'clock, Indy."

"I'll pick you up then," the man said with a smile, and returned to the truck. He backed out of the lane and drove away.

Pete, acting as foreman, got the tree house project under way at once.

With a boost from his big brother and Dave, Ricky shinned up the oak. Upon reaching the topmost branches, he called down, "Here's a great spot for the platform." The boy reported that two stout limbs extended from the tree trunk parallel to the ground. "And there are plenty of leaves up here to hide us," he added.

Pete tossed Ricky one end of the long rope, which the boy tied securely to a branch. The lumber would be tied to the other end and hauled up.

Next Dave cut short lengths of wood. Using hammer and nails, Pete fastened these to the tree trunk like rungs on a ladder. When they were all in place, he and Dave, followed by Pam, climbed into the tree to examine the spot which Ricky had chosen.

"What do you think of it, Pam?" Pete asked his sister.

"It's a good spot," the girl said. "But, Pete, please be careful. It's so high up."

Her brother laughed and promised that the builders would be cautious.

Pam returned to the base of the tree and Jeff climbed up to the boys. It was the girls' job to tie hammers, the bucket of nails, and whatever wood was needed to the end of the rope. The boys hauled up the material and started to work.

By noontime the triangular-shaped platform was nearly half finished. Enough of the boards had been laid so that the boys could sit down and rest for a moment.

"Yikes, what a view!" Ricky said. They could see the countryside around the Antique House and the whole lake. The shore line curved in and out, making little coves and promontories.

"This is a great lookout!" Dave declared. "Say, Pete, what's that big pipe over there?" He pointed far down the lake front, where the outline of a large culvert could be seen.

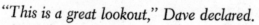
"This is a great lookout," Dave declared.

The Hollister boy explained that the huge pipe, tall enough for a person to walk into, was used to carry storm water from Shoreham and empty it into the lake.

"I've seen it from our motorboat," he added.

"Are you fellows finished?" Holly's voice floated up through the tree branches.

"Not yet," answered Pete.

"Well, come on down for lunch. We're hungry."

While Pete, Dave, and Jeff descended the rungs, Ricky slid down the rope and reached the ground first.

Pam had spread a picnic cloth on the grass. On it were plates containing sandwiches and paper cups brimful of cool milk. The three boys dashed to the side of the lake to wash their hands and were back in a jiffy. Seated cross-legged on the ground, they ate hungrily.

When they had nearly finished, the *putt-putt-putt* of a small motorboat sounded from around the bend in the shore.

"Oh-oh," Pete said. "What if it's those two men?"

"I thought they only showed up in the evening," Dave Mead replied.

"We can't be too sure," Pam put in.

"Let's not take any chances," Pete said. "We'd better hide."

Draining their cups quickly, the children crept into the bushes. Pam, who quickly folded the white cloth and put it into the hamper, was the last to hide, dragging the basket with her.

Putt-putt-putt. The sound of the motor came closer. Then, as the children peered out from the brush, they saw a boat rounding the bend. In it were two figures.

"Are those the same men?" Dave whispered to Pete.

"I don't think so." A moment later he added, relieved, "They're only boys."

The Detective Club members stepped out of hiding.

The girls respread the white cloth and set out cupcakes for dessert. The boys, shielding their eyes from the sun, watched the small craft come nearer to the shore.

"Crickets!" Pete cried out. "It's Will's motorboat."

"Joey Brill's with him!" Jeff piped.

Ricky groaned. "They've seen us. Here they come."

The boat was heading straight toward them. When the bow scraped on the shore, Joey jumped out and pulled it high on the beach while Will tilted the motor.

Joey looked cautiously about to see whether any adults were present. Seeing none, he advanced boldly toward the picnickers. "Quite a party," he remarked. "Exclusive for the Shoreham Detective Club, I guess."

"You can say that," Pete replied.

"Hey, look!" Will exclaimed, pointing up. "They're building a tree house."

Joey squinted up through the leafy branches. "It must be a secret meeting place."

"Here, Joey," Pam put in, trying to divert his attention, "why don't you have some dessert with us? You, too, Will."

Both boys looked surprised at Pam's offer.

"Thanks," Joey said as he accepted the cake, which Pam handed him on a paper plate.

When the two had finished eating, Pete said, "Are you fellows on your way someplace?"

"No place in particular," Joey replied. "I guess we'll hang around and watch you work." He and Will grinned at each other.

When Pete, Dave, and the two younger boys were up in the tree again, Pete said, "I wish those pests would go away."

"I wonder what they're up to," Dave remarked as he hammered busily.

"They'll try something, you can bet that. Hey, Ricky, you and Jeff pull up another board."

They worked hard until the triangular platform was completed and handrails nailed along two sides of it. All the while Joey and Will lay on their backs at the foot of the tree, looking up and making remarks about the builders.

At three o'clock sharp Indy Roades drove The Trading Post truck down the lane. He stepped out, walked over to the oak, and admired the platform.

"All right, let's get your gear loaded," Indy said. "Your dad wants me to return right away."

The Hollisters and their friends picked up the

scraps of wood and, along with the tools and the rope, put them in the back of the truck.

"Sorry to see you go," Joey remarked.

"What are you two going to do?" Pete asked, reluctant to return to Shoreham.

"We're just going to take over this place when you leave," Joey said with a crooked grin.

"Oh no, you won't!" Pete retorted. "This is our tree house."

"It won't be when you leave," Will replied with a snicker.

"Now listen, Joey," Pete said, stepping close to the bully. "I'm not joking. This lookout is very important to us, so don't touch it."

"Oh," Joey crowed, "so that's it! A spying place for your Detective Club!"

Pete bit his lip over the important slip he had made. "Well, call it whatever you want," he said, "but just stay out."

As the Hollisters drove off, Pete looked back and saw the two bullies laughing.

"If Joey fools around that platform, I'll settle with him," he declared.

"If you don't, I will," Dave chimed in. "We worked too hard to have those two spoil our plans."

After supper that evening Pete and Pam discussed the lookout with their parents.

"That sounds like a good idea," Mr. Hollister told his young detectives, "provided you're well camouflaged."

"We will be, Dad," Pete assured his father. "And I have another plan, too."

"What is it?" Pam asked. "You didn't tell me."

Her brother smiled and replied, "It's a surprise. I'm going to have Charles help me to spy on those men if they should appear again. By using Dad's binoculars we can see their faces and also hear what they're saying."

"With binoculars?" Mrs. Hollister asked with a puzzled expression.

"That's where Charles comes in," the boy replied. "He'll be able to read their lips!"

"Oh, Pete, what a brilliant idea," Pam declared.

"Pretty clever," Mr. Hollister agreed. "I hope it works out, son."

An hour later, when it began to get dark, Mrs. Hollister stepped onto the porch and called her children, who had been playing in the yard.

Pete and Pam came running in. Ricky and Holly, however, were not around. Neither was Sue.

"Where are those children!" Mrs. Hollister said. "Zip, did you see them?" she asked the collie as he raced in behind Pete and Pam.

Zip whimpered and barked sharply.

"He knows something," Pam declared.

"Maybe they're at Donna's," Pete suggested.

Pam telephoned the Martins' house, and the plump little girl reported that she had seen the missing children a half hour before. Holly and Ricky were on their bicycles, and Sue was riding in Ricky's carrier basket.

As Pam hung up, her eyes brightened. "Mother!" she declared. "I'll bet I know where they went."

"Where?"

"To the tree house! Remember, Sue hasn't seen it yet. She probably begged to go."

"You may be right, Pam," her mother said. "Daddy can drive us out there before it gets too dark."

Moments later Mr. and Mrs. Hollister and the two older children were speeding along the road toward the lookout. The tree toads were already chirping a merry tune by the time Mr. Hollister drove down the old lane and arrived at the shore front.

"I see their bikes!" Pete cried out as he ran toward the big tree.

"And there's Sue!" Mrs. Hollister called out. She hurried after her son.

When the little girl saw the four approaching, she waved her arms and cried out in a shrill voice. "Mommy, Daddy, save them! Save them!"

CHAPTER 13

NIGHT SLEUTHING

PETE sprinted faster and was first to arrive beneath the oak tree. He glanced up and, in the dim light, saw that the middle boards in the platform had been removed.

Then, as his eyes grew accustomed to the darkness, he noticed two forms struggling frantically.

One was Ricky. The boy was lying flat on the remaining boards. His arms were extended down through the hole. Both his hands grasped Holly's wrists. With small cries of fright, she was trying to climb back up.

"Hold on!" Pete cried out. He scrambled up the wooden rungs until he was just beneath the lookout.

Steadying himself against the tree trunk, the boy took a step out on a strong branch below and behind his sister. Reaching out, he wrapped his right arm around the girl's waist. "Let go now, Ricky!" he cried.

The sudden drop of Holly's weight nearly pulled Pete from the limb. But, using all his strength, he swung himself and his sister against the trunk of the oak tree, where they clung.

Trembling, both of them sank into the crotch of the huge branch to catch their breath.

"Hurray!" Sue cried from below.

"Oh, Pete, that was so brave," his mother called.

"Good boy!" Mr. Hollister boomed.

When Holly had recovered from her fright, she climbed down to the ground. Pete followed, and Ricky was the last to alight from the tree house.

"Goodness, what happened?" Mrs. Hollister asked as she hugged Holly tightly to her.

"Somebody ripped a few floor boards off our platform," Ricky explained. He said that he and Holly had ridden Sue out to see the new project. When the older children had climbed up, they had not noticed the missing planks because of the darkness. Holly had plunged through and would have fallen to the ground if her brother had not caught hold of her wrist.

As the family walked back to the car, Pam quietly asked Pete, "Do you think Joey and Will did this trick?"

"Probably," Pete replied grimly, remembering how they had left the two standing under the tree that afternoon.

After the boys stowed the two bicycles in the back of the station wagon, the Hollisters set off for home.

On the way Pete said he was going to call Charles and ask him to ride out to the tree house the next evening. "We can repair the floor," he said, "and spy on the two men if they turn up."

As soon as they arrived in the house, Pete telephoned the Johnson farm. He told the farmer of his plan and asked if he would give the message to Charles.

"But he's not here," the man said.

Pete frowned and looked alarmed. "Where is he?" he asked.

"Charles went to the city, and I don't know when he'll be back," the farmer replied. He explained that someone in the deaf boy's family had become ill. A telegram had come urging him to come home immediately.

Pete thanked Mr. Johnson and said good-by. When he told his family what had happened, they looked troubled.

"That poor boy," Mrs. Hollister said. "I hope that whoever is sick recovers quickly."

"So do I," Pete said. "This ruins my spying plans, too," he added glumly. It seemed to him for a moment that the work of the Detective Club might come to a standstill.

Suddenly the telephone rang. Pete answered it. Dave was on the line and spoke excitedly. "I'm at the Antique House," he said. "There have been more funny noises over here tonight. And guess what? Mrs. Neeley says that we may explore this place after dark."

"When?" Pete asked.

"Right now. Tonight. Can you come over? If so, you don't need a flashlight. I have my big one."

Pete put the palm of his hand over the mouthpiece and asked his parents. At first Mrs. Hollister was reluctant to allow the children to explore the old

It was spookier than ever at night.

mansion at night. All of them pleaded, however, and finally she said, "All right. Pete and Pam may go, but you must take Zip with you."

"Oh, thank you, Mother!" Pam exclaimed, hugging her.

Mr. Hollister offered to drive his son and daughter to the place, but Pete said that their bicycles had good lights and that they would pedal over by themselves.

The two children started off toward Serpentine Road, with Zip bounding along behind them.

When they arrived at the gatehouse, they found Dave outside, eager to go. In his hands he held a long silver flashlight with a large lens.

The Hollisters parked their bicycles as Zip trotted around, sniffing here and there with an excited air of expectancy.

"O.K., let's get on with the search," Dave said. He led the way up the drive to the Antique House. The broad beam of the flashlight carved a path through the darkness, and soon the children stood at the front entrance. Pam grasped Zip's collar and held the dog close to her side. Pete quietly turned the knob and opened the great oaken door. They all stepped inside.

"Crickets! This is spookier than ever at night," Pete whispered.

The children listened quietly. There was not a sound.

Now Dave led the way with his flashlight and they

entered a small study at one end of the long living room.

As Dave's light played over the shelves of old books, a deep rumbling filled the house. The young detectives froze and listened. Zip's ears stood up in two sharp points and he gave a throaty growl.

From upstairs there came barks and snarls. Pam seized Zip's collar. "There's a dog up there!" she whispered.

"Sounds like a big one," Dave said uneasily. "He might be dangerous."

"But we have Zip to protect us," Pete replied as the dog strained to get away from Pam. Just then there was a sharp bark from above. Zip broke away, dashed into the living room, and bounded up the stairs. Pete, Dave, and Pam raced behind him.

Trying to take three steps at a time, Dave stumbled and banged his flashlight into the banister.

Crash! Darkness! The tinkling sound of glass told the young sleuths that the big flashlight had broken.

The three frightened children stood on the staircase and listened. They could hear Zip dashing from room to room on the third floor. But there were no more sounds of barking.

"G-gollee," Dave said. "Maybe there wasn't any dog up there, after all."

"Crickets!" Pete exclaimed softly. "If we could only find a light."

"I saw a candle mold on the balcony the other day," his sister remembered. "There were several candles lying beside it."

They felt their way up the remaining steps to the landing. With Pam leading, they tiptoed in the darkness to the staircase leading to the third floor. At the foot of it she fumbled until she found a low table and on it the antique mold. Beside the mold were three candles and a matchbook.

Pam opened the flap and felt only three matches. Her fingers trembled as she struck the first one. The glow cast three long shadows across the balcony as she picked up a candle. But her hand was shaking so that the flame flicked out.

"Be careful, Pam," her brother warned. "There are only two left."

This time Pete held the tallow while his sister struck the second light. As she was about to touch it to the candle, Zip dashed downstairs and brushed past her skirts, causing her to bump the match into the wick. The flame went out.

"Only one left!" Pam whispered nervously. "You boys try it this time."

Dave held the candle. Pete struck the match and cupped it in his hands. But as he held it to the candle a strong, cool draft came down the stairs. The light flickered and died.

CHAPTER 14

BANG!

WHEN the last match went out, the place was cloaked in darkness once more.

"What luck!" Pete declared.

"Where did that wind come from?" Dave whispered.

"I don't know," Pete replied, and reached out to find his sister. "Give me your hand," he said to her. "We have to be careful that we don't fall down the stairs getting out of here."

Slowly they felt their way along the balcony. Suddenly the silence was split by a loud hiss. It was followed by rattles, coughs, growls, and then chuckles.

"Good night! What's that?" Dave Mead exclaimed as he fumbled to find the first step and the banister at the same time.

As fast as they could, they made their way down.

Still hand in hand, Pete and Pam hurried across the living room. In the darkness the girl stumbled against a table and fell with a crash.

She was more frightened than hurt. As Pete helped his sister to sit up, her hand rested on an odd-shaped object made of iron. Pam's fingers traced its shape.

"Pete!" she exclaimed. "I think I found the old

boot scraper. This feels like a flat-backed elephant!"

"Come on," Dave urged. "Let's get out of here! Talk later!"

Pam scrambled to her feet and the three children threaded their way across the room. Pete pulled the big door open and they stepped out into the black night. Hastening down the drive, they were relieved to see a light in the gatehouse.

When they knocked on the door, Mrs. Neeley let them in. Pete quickly told her about Pam's fall, and the children took turns examining the iron object.

"Yes, it's a boot scraper," she told them, "but it's been used as a book end long as I can remember."

"Where did you get it?" Pete asked.

"It was in the Antique House when I inherited it," the woman said.

"Did it come from there originally or from somewhere else?" Dave put in.

"I don't know. Why do you ask?"

"This may solve another mystery for us," Pam said, and told the elderly woman about Kerry Flip.

When she had finished, Pete said, "That was quite a scare we got tonight." He related all that had happened.

Mrs. Neeley sat silent, shaking her head.

"What do you think made the noises?" Dave asked uneasily.

"It could have been a barn owl," Pete replied. "They make all those odd sounds."

The children looked at each other doubtfully.

"Terrible!" Mrs. Neeley exclaimed suddenly. "To think that the ghost blew out your last match!"

"It was just a draft, I'm sure," Pam said, not sounding very certain.

"No, no, no, no!" Mrs. Neeley said, shaking her head on each word. "This is the end!" She told the children they would have to give up their investigation of the Antique House. "I'll sell it, that's what I'll do," she said, "and go somewhere far away. And you, Pam, may keep the old boot scraper."

"Please don't go," Pam said.

"We'll see it through," Pete assured her. The children explained that there was some trickery going on. Just what, they had not found out yet.

"If you give us a little more time," Pete urged, "I'm sure we can unhaunt this place for you, Mrs. Neeley."

After the elderly woman finally agreed to give the young detectives another chance, they returned to their bicycles, switched on their running lights, and pedaled down Serpentine Road. Pete took a backward glance at the old mansion, and a chill ran down his back as he saw a light flicker off and on in a third-floor room.

Next morning Pam showed the flat-backed elephant to Holly, Ricky, and Sue.

"Yikes!" the freckle-faced boy exclaimed. "That's a good clue. Where do you think it'll lead, Pam?"

"It can't lead anywhere," Holly said, twirling one of her pigtails.

"What do you mean?" Pete asked.

His sister explained that if the boot scraper had been removed from the old doorway, perhaps the entrance itself no longer existed.

"Crickets!" Pete said, snapping his fingers. "Holly's right. Why didn't we think of that!"

"No wonder we couldn't find it if it's gone," Pam said ruefully.

"Maybe it was torn down or covered up," Ricky commented.

The older girl shook her head and sighed. "That'll make it harder than ever to locate the house where Kerry Flip's mother lived," she said.

While the others thought it over glumly, Ricky walked across the room balancing the boot scraper on his head. When he reached the telephone, it rang; he picked it up, holding his neck stiff.

"Oh, hello, Mr. Fundy," he said, and the elephant fell off. He listened for a few minutes, then said, "Yes, sir! Right away!"

"What does Mr. Fundy want?" Pete asked.

"He says it's very important," Ricky answered, "and he wants to see us immediately."

Pete said that he could not go because he and Dave had planned to rebuild the floor of their lookout platform.

"All right," Pam said. "The rest of us will call on him."

After getting a hammer and nails, Pete jumped on his bike and set off for Dave's place. At the same time Pam, Holly, and Ricky started for Mr. Fundy's home.

They met the old gentleman at the front door.

"Come in, children," he said kindly. "I may be able to help you solve one of your mysteries."

"Kerry Flip's, do you mean?" Ricky asked excitedly as they followed the photographer into the living room.

The elderly man nodded his white head. "If my memory serves me correctly, I think I took that old picture."

"Oh!" Pam declared. "How wonderful!"

"I still might have the negative," Mr. Fundy went on, his eyes looking sleepier than ever. "And if I do, it will show the house Mr. Flip's mother lived in."

"Yikes!" Ricky shouted. "Let's find it!"

The photographer said that that would not be easy. He had thousands of negatives in the cellar room where Ricky had fallen through the window.

"It might take days to unearth it," the old man said.

"I have an idea!" Pam declared. "We'll get all the girls in our Detective Club to help look through your files, Mr. Fundy."

"Excellent!" he replied. "Come over any time."

While he and Pam were talking, Holly and Ricky sidled into the adjoining studio and glanced about. In a moment the old gentleman escorted Pam in to show her around.

High up on a shelf the red-haired boy saw an odd-looking contraption. It was a piece of metal attached to a handle.

"What's that, Mr. Fundy?" he asked.

The photographer chuckled. "It's an old powder flash gun."

"Could you take our picture with it?"

"If you don't mind the noise."

"We won't," chorused Ricky and Holly.

Mr. Fundy rummaged through a drawer and came upon a metal box. Opening it, he said, "If this old powder works, we'll have a picture."

He arranged the three children on a bench before a large camera, which stood on a tripod. Next, he put a black cloth back over his head and adjusted the focus. Then he sprinkled flash powder on the crosspiece of the antique flash gun.

Holding the handle in his right hand, he put his finger to a wire trigger and said, "All right, look into the camera."

Just as Pam, Ricky, and Holly obeyed, there was a terrific *boom* and the whole room lighted up.

Ricky fell backward over the bench and landed on the floor. As the white smoke drifted away he picked himself up, looking sheepish.

"That scared me, Mr. Fundy!" Ricky admitted, and his sisters laughed.

"Wait till Pete sees this picture!" Pam said as Mr. Fundy began to develop it.

Pete, by this time, was far away and engaged in a different kind of adventure. He had called for Dave,

There was a terrific boom.

and together they had ridden to their tree house, each balancing a board on the handle bars.

They climbed the rungs with the planks under their arms, reached the platform, and quickly repaired it.

Pete gazed along the shore from their high perch. "There's one thing we may have overlooked, Dave."

"What's that?"

"The culvert. It's big enough for a person to walk into. Maybe that's where those two men disappeared."

"Let's investigate it," Dave said.

They clambered out of the tree house and reached the ground just as two other cyclists sped down the lane and skidded to a stop near the oak tree.

"Will and Joey!" Dave exclaimed.

The two boys stepped off their bicycles as Pete strode toward them.

"I want to talk to you, Joey," he said.

"What about?"

"Who ripped the boards off our tree house?"

"I did," Joey bragged, "so——"

He never got to finish his sentence, because Pete gave him such a hard thump that he rolled onto the ground. The blow took the bully by surprise. He scrambled to his feet, apologizing.

Will explained that it was Joey's idea to play bomber and drop stones down through the opening in the platform.

"I ought to punch you in the nose, too," Pete

said, and told him about the danger to Ricky and Holly.

Will hung his head. He did not want to fight. "All right," he muttered, "we won't do it again."

"Just make sure you don't," Dave remarked. He added, "Now scram and stay away from our tree house."

"We want to help you solve your mystery," Joey said. "We won't bother your lookout again, honest."

Pete and Dave exchanged a look. If they refused the bullies' aid, they might follow and make trouble.

"All right," the Hollister boy said. "You can come with us, but you'll have to do as we tell you."

As the four boys walked along the lake front, the Detective Club members explained that they were going to investigate the culvert. After more than half a mile, they turned a bend and approached a cove.

There was the huge pipe. It opened near the water's edge, and from it came a small trickle.

"We're going to look inside here," Pete told their unwelcome companions, pointing into the dark mouth of the culvert.

"If you really want to come with us, O.K.," Dave said.

"But you'd better take thick sticks along," Pete warned them. "You never can tell what you'll find in a place like this."

"Or what'll find you," Dave added.

While Joey and Will picked up stout weapons, Pete flashed a finger-alphabet message to his friend: "See clues, say nothing. Come out. Go back later."

The other boy nodded.

Pete led the way into the big pipe, followed by Dave and Will with Joey last. After the hot, bright sunlight, the boys could hardly see in the gloom. It was cool and smelled dank. The bottom was covered with silt and mossy stones.

Pete walked on ahead. "Be careful," he advised them. "It's slippery." His voice sounded hollow.

They had gone in about thirty paces when suddenly Pete stepped on something soft. It squirmed under his foot.

CHAPTER 15

THE TATTLETALE

With a squeak of fright, a muskrat wriggled away and ran out of the tunnel.

While Pete watched it scurry off, Joey and Will pressed deeper into the culvert.

"Wait for us," Dave commanded.

"What's the matter? You afraid we'll find some clues before you do?" Joey retorted.

Before Pete and Dave could catch up, they heard Will cry out, "Hey, look at this—an opening in the side of the pipe!" The echoing footsteps faded as Joey stopped to investigate.

Suddenly they heard him yelp. He raced past them toward the mouth of the culvert, with Will close behind. "There's something in there!" Joey called back. "I saw it move!"

Pete and Dave did not run. Cautiously they moved ahead to peer into the dark hole in the side of the big concrete pipe. Even in the gloom they could see that the opening was about five feet high and three feet wide.

The boys stopped to listen. Nothing could be heard except drops of water, which slowly fell somewhere inside the black hole.

"It might be a tunnel," Pete said. "Let's go in."

"Careful," Dave warned. "It's pretty dark."

Pete stepped forward, feeling along the sides of the hole with his hands.

"Crickets!" he whispered to Dave. "It's a tunnel all right, and it's lined with bricks."

He advanced two steps more and reached over his head. The blocks in the arched ceiling of the tunnel were loose. One fell down, hitting him on the foot.

"What if the whole thing falls in on us?" Dave said. "I don't think we ought to go any farther."

His friend had to agree, although he did not like to give up the exploration. They felt their way back into the culvert and walked toward the mouth of it.

"What luck," Pete grumbled, "having Joey and Will stumble on such a good clue."

"They'll probably spread the story," Dave said, "and everyone will be down here gawking around."

"It'll spoil our chance to solve the case," Pete went on. "I have a hunch that old tunnel might lead to the Antique House. Maybe that's how the ghost is getting in and out without being seen. If people know about it, he'll be scared off."

The two chums emerged, blinking, into the daylight again.

"What did you find out?" asked Joey, who was waiting for them. "Is it a tunnel?"

"Where does it lead?" Will interrupted.

"What was moving in there?" Joey went on.

"I don't know," Pete replied. Then, in a serious

voice, he added, "Listen, fellows, let's not spread the news around."

"O.K.," Joey said glibly. "You know us. We can keep a secret, can't we, Will?"

"If you do," the Hollister boy promised, "we'll tell you all about what we find in that tunnel."

On the way back to town, Dave invited Pete to have lunch at his house.

"Thank you," the boy replied. "I'd like to." Then he added, "You know, there's something we ought to do this afternoon."

"What's that?"

Pete told his friend that the town engineer of Shoreham was the man in charge of culverts and storm sewers.

"Maybe he knows something about the old tunnel," he said.

"We'll go see him right after lunch," the other boy replied enthusiastically.

Dave Mead lived with his parents in a pleasant one-story house. His mother, who used to be a cooking teacher in the Shoreham Junior High School, was busy in the kitchen making chocolate éclairs.

"I'm so glad you came for lunch, Pete," Mrs. Mead said with a big smile. "You both look kind of hungry, and I have just the thing—roast beef sandwiches." The woman prepared two plates for the boys. "If you'll wait for another half hour, I'll have éclairs ready for you," she promised.

"But, Mrs. Mead," Pete said, "we have to——"

Dave's mother beamed and said positively, "Whatever you boys have to do must wait for this dessert. I know you'll like it."

"They're super!" Dave agreed. "We'd better stick around."

Although the meat was tasty, Pete could not keep his mind on what he was eating. Exploring the tunnel seemed urgent if they were to solve the riddle of the haunted house. How long could Will and Joey keep the secret? he asked himself. Maybe not at all!

As the two boys finished their lunch, Mrs. Mead carefully put the warm éclairs in the refrigerator to cool. Pete tried not to fidget while he waited. Finally the woman served them.

"Umm-yum! They're delicious!" Pete exclaimed. "Dave, you were right. Thank you, Mrs. Mead."

After eating two chocolate éclairs apiece, the boys mounted their bicycles again and rode into the center of Shoreham. Not far from the business section was the municipal plaza. On one side was the Shoreham High School and library. Facing them across a broad quadrangle was the municipal building.

The boys raced up the stone steps and entered the cool corridor. There the elevator operator told them that the town engineer was located on the second floor. "His name is Mr. Cramer," the man said as Pete and Dave stepped off the elevator.

They walked down the hall until they came to a door marked "Shoreham Town Engineer." After entering, they found themselves in a large room. The walls were hung with charts and maps, and along one side several men were seated at drawing boards.

One of them rose and walked over. "Is there something I can do for you fellows?"

"We're looking for Mr. Cramer," Pete said.

"I'm your man," came the reply.

Pete had expected to see an older person. The town engineer was about his father's age, not quite so tall, and very slender. He had black wavy hair and wore glasses.

"We've come on some secret business," Dave told him.

"In that case," the man said, "come into my private office."

He led the boys through another door to a small room. In it were a desk, several chairs, and filing cabinets.

"It's about that big culvert on the lake shore near the Antique House," Pete began, after they had taken seats.

"That's a storm sewer," Mr. Cramer said. "We installed it several years ago to carry off rain water in the northern part of town."

"Did you help to put it in?" Pete asked.

"Yes. I was assistant engineer at that time." The man smiled. "What's your secret?"

Pete told about finding the tunnel leading into the culvert. Mr. Cramer frowned.

"Yes. I remember that passageway," he said. "We bisected it when we put the big pipe through—cut it right in half."

"Does it lead to the Antique House?" Dave asked eagerly.

The engineer leaned back in his swivel chair. "I suppose so," he replied. "There's no place else nearby for it to go to. Many of those old houses had underground entrances."

"Didn't you follow the tunnel?" Pete asked, amazed.

The man smiled. "For a little way, but the bricks were crumbling and it was risky. Besides, I was too busy on the culvert to take time out."

Mr. Cramer then thanked the boys for telling him of their discovery. As he escorted them to the door he added, "First thing Monday morning I'll send a repair crew out to close up the break-through into the passageway. Meantime, you fellows stay away from there."

Outside the engineer's office, the two boys looked at each other in dismay.

"What a mistake this was!" Pete exclaimed. "When the workmen close the hole, that'll surely scare off the 'ghost.'"

"Unless we catch him before then," Dave said as they rang for the elevator.

"But today's Friday," Pete reminded him. "It doesn't give us much time. And now Charles is gone, just when I counted on him to help us."

They rode down to the first floor, left the building, picked up their bikes, and pedaled home in worried silence.

When they reached Dave's street, Pete spoke. "The worst of it is—Mr. Cramer didn't tell us anything we didn't know already."

"Didn't you follow the tunnel?" Pete asked.

The boys said good-by and Pete continued home.

As he turned into his driveway, what he saw made his sober face break into a wide grin. Seated on the grass with Pam and Ricky and Jeff Hunter was Charles Belden.

Pete jumped from his bike and ran over, but before he could say a word Pam asked him, "Did you hear the news?"

"What news?" he asked, noting their serious faces.

"Joey and Will discovered a secret tunnel in the culvert by the Antique House," Ricky burst out.

"They're telling everybody," Jeff piped up. "I heard it from the new soda boy in the drugstore. They told him how they explored it."

"They did not!" Pete exclaimed hotly, and told the others what really had happened, including the visit to the town engineer. "Now we haven't even got until Monday to solve the mystery!" he exploded.

"If the 'ghost' hears about this or sees children hanging around there, he'll stay away," Pam agreed.

"Maybe he has heard it and is gone already," Ricky said gloomily.

Pete's eye fell on Charles, who was sitting quietly trying to read their lips.

"Crickets," he said, "am I glad to see you!" The deaf boy caught the words and smiled.

Quickly Pete spelled out the story for him, and then asked where he had been. Charles said that his grandfather had been sick but was better now, so that he had been able to come back to Johnson's farm.

Then he handed Pete a photograph he had been holding. It showed Pam, Holly, and Ricky seated on a bench in Mr. Fundy's studio.

"Your eyes certainly are wide!" Pete said to his brother. "Looks like you've seen a ghost."

"You should have been there when that powder flash gun went off!" Ricky replied, and told how he had taken a back flip.

Pete was heartened to learn of Mr. Fundy's recollection of the old photo.

"When are you going to look through the negatives?" he asked.

"Maybe tonight," Pam answered.

Pete agreed that it was a good sleuthing job for girls to do, because it took so much patience. Then, moving his fingers deftly, he asked Charles to accompany him to their tree lookout that evening.

"All right," the boy replied. He arranged to meet Pete there at six o'clock.

During supper Pete asked permission to borrow his father's binoculars and Mr. Hollister said yes. As soon as the boy had finished eating, he slung the black leather case containing the glasses around his neck and set off.

Charles was waiting for him at the foot of the oak tree.

The two friends climbed to the platform and looked out over Pine Lake. A few boats churned back and forth. But there was nobody on the shore in this out-of-the-way place.

The boys took turns watching the culvert with the powerful binoculars. An hour passed.

"Nobody's coming," Pete said in finger language.

Charles shrugged his shoulders. Then he pointed to the horizon, where dark clouds were gathering. Moments later Pete heard a peal of thunder from far across the water. Flashes of lightning flicked out like snake tongues.

"A storm is coming," Charles communicated.

Pete nodded. And a big one at that, he thought uneasily. How long could they afford to wait? In a few more minutes, when the lightning moved closer, the tree would be unsafe.

Just as the two boys were about to climb down, two men appeared as if by magic near the mouth of the culvert. Through his glasses Pete could see the back of one man's head and the face of another. They were talking.

Quickly Pete passed the binoculars to his friend and asked, "What are they saying?"

Charles pressed the glasses to his eyes and peered intently at the strangers.

CHAPTER 16

LOST IS FOUND

THE deaf boy studied the two men carefully. The one facing the lookout where the boys were spying was tall and thin. He had a long neck and a small round head. Thick black hair grew low on his forehead. The man with his back toward them was short, broad-shouldered, and powerfully built.

Charles put down the binoculars for a moment and communicated with Pete. The tall stranger had said, "Those kids are getting too nosy. What'll we do now?"

"So they're on to us!" Pete exclaimed. "What was the reply?"

His friend told him that the stocky man did not turn his head so he could not see what the answer was.

"If we only knew what they were planning," Pete said, "we might act to foil them."

Charles put the binoculars to his eyes again. The men had moved behind some bushes and were gone.

Just then the spattering of rain on the leaves overhead told the young sleuths that the storm had finally arrived. Moments later a steady downpour turned

Pine Lake into a sheet of white froth. The lightning grew more intense.

Both boys realized that the tall oak was now too dangerous a place.

Swiftly they climbed down and reached the ground just as a high wind ripped through the top of the tree. It swayed violently, and several boards from their platform were torn loose and sailed into the brush.

"Crickets!" Pete cried. "That was a narrow escape!"

In spite of the drenching rain, the companions decided to dash for home. Both were wringing wet anyhow.

Charles waved and trotted off toward the Johnson farm. Pete pedaled furiously and soon raced into his own driveway. After putting his bike in the garage, he hastened inside the house. Mr. Hollister and Ricky were alone in the living room.

"Excuse me," Pete said, handing the binoculars to his brother as he hurried past. "I've got to change." He ran upstairs to his room and returned a few minutes later in dry clothes to find Ricky wiping the black leather case.

Pete related what had happened and then asked, "Where is everybody?"

His father told him that Mrs. Hollister and all the girls of the Detective Club had gone to Mr. Fundy's home shortly after supper.

"Crickets, they've been there a long time," Pete remarked.

Mr. Hollister and his two sons discussed the mystery of the two men on the beach. They decided to tell Officer Cal about it the next day. An hour passed. Ricky yawned sleepily, then looked out the front window for a while, resting his nose against the glass.

"Yikes!" he said finally. "Do you suppose something has happened to Mother and the girls?"

As if in answer, two headlights shone and the station wagon turned in the drive.

It was still raining hard, and the girls dashed up the front steps onto the porch.

"We found it! We found it!" Holly screamed as she opened the door and burst into the living room.

"The old negative?" Pete asked.

"Hurray!" Pam shouted, and threw her arms about her father. Little Sue skipped in ahead of her mother. Then the three girls joined hands and danced about Mrs. Hollister as if she were a Maypole. Pete, Ricky, and their father looked on, bewildered.

Seeing their faces, the woman chuckled and said, "Come now, let's calm down and tell the boys all about it."

The three excited children threw themselves on the sofa, their faces flushed with happiness.

"Who said girls aren't good detectives!" Holly crowed.

"We've solved the mystery!" Pam declared.

"Well, yikes! Tell us about it!" Ricky protested. "And quit puffing."

Mrs. Hollister reached into her large purse and

They danced around their mother.

pulled out an eight-by-ten-inch photograph. Her husband and the boys pressed around her.

"Mr. Fundy took this picture years ago," Mrs. Hollister said.

"It's the Antique House!" Pete exclaimed.

"And, look, there's the missing doorway!" Ricky said excitedly.

"It must have been covered up by construction in later years," Mr. Hollister ventured.

"That's exactly what Mr. Fundy said," Pam put in.

"I'm going to call Kerry Flip right away," Holly declared, and dashed across the room toward the telephone.

"Oh no, it's too late," Pam objected. "We'll tell him in the morning."

"So that's where Kerry Flip's mother lived," Pete said. "And to think the old house was right under our noses all the time." Then his mouth opened slowly and he looked from one girl to the other. "Say!" he exploded. "Kerry's mother and Mrs. Neeley are relatives!"

"What do you suppose we were dancing for?" Holly said impishly.

"Of course!" Pam declared joyously. "And Kerry's related to Mrs. Neeley."

"You girls certainly are detectives!" their father said. "I've got a regular police department right in my own home!"

Pam beamed and Holly giggled, but Sue was very quiet, being fast asleep on the sofa. Pete carried the little girl upstairs and Pam tucked her into her bed.

Mrs. Hollister, meanwhile, prepared cocoa and cookies for her excited adventurers. After they had eaten every crumb, they trooped reluctantly up to bed, hardly able to wait until the next morning, when they could tell Kerry Flip the good news.

The children arose early, and even before breakfast Pam telephoned the acrobat. While the others crowded around her, she told him of their discovery.

"I can't believe it!" Kerry Flip said. "It's wonderful!"

Pam laughed. "It's really true," she said. "Mrs. Neeley must be part of your family."

Kerry replied that it was amazing what the Hollisters had done. He promised to ride over to the gatehouse immediately.

"Good-by," Pam said, "and good luck."

While she told her brothers and sisters word for word what Kerry had said, the delicious smell of frying bacon drifted from the kitchen. The girls went to help their mother, and in a few minutes the family was seated around the table.

Mr. Hollister told his sons that he had a job for them to do at The Trading Post that morning.

"Some crates of rustic furniture have arrived from the West Coast," he said. "I'm depending on you boys to unpack them."

Although Pete wanted to go to the shore to see if he could find a trace of the two men, he told his father he would gladly help. First, however, he tried to call Officer Cal. The desk sergeant who answered said the young policeman would be on duty in another hour.

"I'll get in touch with him later," Pete said, disappointed. He knew that the time left to solve the mystery was running out.

Mr. Hollister drove his sons to the store. In back of the place stood a dozen packing cases, and the boys went to work immediately. Using a hammer and a pinch bar, they ripped the slatted crates apart and carried the furniture into the store.

When the job was finished, Ricky and Pete stacked the wood neatly to one side and swept up the excelsior which was scattered about.

"That's fine," Mr. Hollister said. "Now here are some letters I'd like you to drop in the postbox. Then your work is done."

He handed Pete a bundle of envelopes which advertised a sale to be held at Mr. Hollister's store. The brothers hastened down the street and deposited them in a mailbox.

As they were hurrying home, Ricky spied Joey Brill. The boy was standing on the opposite corner talking to a tall man. Pete stopped short and stared at the two.

"Ricky!" Pete said, the words nearly choking in his throat. "That's one of the men we spied on yesterday!"

Joey and the stranger had not seen the brothers. The man obviously was asking questions, and the boy was answering them.

"What'll we do, Pete?" Ricky asked.

"Run down to the police station and get Officer Cal. He should be there now."

The red-haired lad dashed off toward the municipal building while Pete sauntered across the street toward the pair on the corner. Would this man recognize him? Pete wondered. The tall fellow glanced at the boy but continued to chat.

Pete moved close to Joey and whispered, "Don't tell him anything. I think he's——"

The bully wheeled around to face Pete. In a loud voice he said, "Mind your own business! I don't care about your old Detective Club."

Hearing this, the man backed off. He turned and hurried down the street, his long legs moving faster and faster.

Pete started after him, but Joey barred his way. Then the Hollister boy saw Ricky and Officer Cal far down the block.

"That's the man! Get him, Cal!" Pete cried out.

When the stranger saw the policeman running toward him, he turned again and fled in the direction of the two boys.

"Let me go!" Pete cried, trying to shove the bully aside. "Can't you see that man's a crook!"

The runner was almost upon them.

With a sudden hard push, Pete rocked Joey back on his heels. Turning, he flung himself in the path of the fugitive. His shoulder hit the running man's knees. With a cry of alarm, the fellow crashed to the sidewalk.

CHAPTER 17

THE SECRET ROOM

THE sprawling man was hauled to his feet by Officer Cal. After slipping handcuffs on him, the policeman said, "What's your name?"

"I won't talk," came the surly reply.

"We'll see about that at the police station," the officer replied. He turned to Pete. "Good work," he said. "Great football blocking!" Then he asked Joey Brill to come along with Pete and Ricky as a witness.

"I—I didn't do anything wrong," Joey stammered.

"I know that," Officer Cal assured the frightened boy. "But you may be able to help us."

At headquarters the prisoner's wallet was examined and the name Horace Neman found on an identification card. Then the questioning began.

"What were you talking to Joey Brill about?" Officer Cal queried.

"I was asking directions!"

"That's not true," Joey spoke up. He said the man had offered him a quarter if he would visit the Shoreham Jewelry Store and find out what time the manager went to lunch.

The prisoner scowled. "Don't you believe it," he said. "The kid's balmy!"

"I think he's telling the truth," Officer Cal remarked. "Neman, I'm looking for a gang of gem thieves and I'm holding you on suspicion."

"May I say something, please?" Pete asked.

"Go right ahead."

The tall man shifted uncomfortably as the boy looked him straight in the eye.

"What were you doing on the shore of Pine Lake near the Antique House last night?" Pete asked.

"I don't know what you're talking about," Neman replied.

"Did you send us a threatening note?" Pete continued.

The man looked at him disdainfully. "Why, I don't even know your name."

The boy saw it was no use to go on questioning.

In spite of his protests, Horace Neman's fingerprints were taken and checked against local police records. It was discovered that he had committed petty thefts around Shoreham many years before.

As the prisoner was led away to a cell, Cal took Pete aside and said, "Mr. Cramer told me of your report. In a day or so, when the storm water has drained out of the culvert, we'll go in and investigate the old tunnel."

Pete thanked the officer, and the three boys left the police station. Joey ran away from the Hollisters without a word, and they went directly home for lunch.

There they found Kerry Flip talking excitedly with their mother and sisters in the living room. "Pete,

Ricky," the acrobat cried out happily, "guess what! Mrs. Neeley is my Great-aunt Dolly."

"She was his grandmother's youngest sister," Pam explained.

"Yikes, how do you know that?" Ricky asked.

The young man told them that Mrs. Neeley had compared pictures of her niece in her family album with his old photo.

"The little girls were one and the same," Pam said happily.

Kerry had learned from the elderly woman that his mother had married an acrobat named Peter Flippenberg and had gone to Europe with him, against her family's wishes.

"There was a terrible misunderstanding," the man said with a sigh, "and nobody wrote letters."

Then he brightened and continued cheerily. "Aunt Dolly wants me to stay here and help her run the Antique House, provided the Hollisters get rid of the ghosts."

"We'll do it!" Pete declared vigorously.

Mrs. Hollister shook her head and said sadly, "Pete, you and the Detective Club members have tried so hard. I think it's time you turned everything over to the police."

"Please, Mother," Pete begged, "we'd like one last try—an overnight stay in the Antique House."

The very idea startled Mrs. Hollister. "Overnight!" she exclaimed. "I wouldn't allow you to do such a dangerous thing."

"But, Mother," Pam said, upholding her brother's

idea, "nighttime is when all the strange things happen."

"Besides," Ricky joined in, "the spook has Pam's shoe. She has to get it back."

Sensing the keen disappointment of the young detectives, Kerry Flip spoke up. "I think your children have a good idea, Mrs. Hollister. If I accompany them, may Pete and Pam spend the night in the haunted house?"

Mrs. Hollister thought hard for a few moments. Then her worried look relaxed. "If you go with them, Mr. Flip, yes."

Instantly she was smothered with hugs and kisses.

"We'll stay there tonight!" Pete exulted.

Kerry Flip had lunch with the Hollisters. When the jolly meal was over, Pete and Pam took naps so that they would not fall asleep during their sleuthing.

That night, at nine o'clock, the young man called for them.

"If you run into any trouble," their father advised, "telephone me or the police; and don't take any unnecessary chances."

He gave flashlights to his two children and their friend, adding, "Use our station wagon, Kerry. I won't need it tonight."

The acrobat drove toward the Antique House with Pete and Pam beside him on the front seat. The sky was dark, and the moon and stars were hidden by low clouds.

For a while they rode along in silence, but as they

turned into Serpentine Road a strange noise sounded from the back of the car.

Startled, Pete turned about in time to see the top of someone's head disappear behind the rear seat.

"Kerry, stop!" Pete commanded. When the station wagon halted, the boy turned on the ceiling light, climbed into the rear seat, and looked behind it.

Two heads popped up, giggling.

"Ricky! Holly!" Pete exclaimed. "What are you doing here?"

"We thought you were home in bed!" Pam declared. "Does Mother know you came along?"

"No. We're stowaways," Holly said with an impish grin.

"We want to help you unhaunt the mansion," Ricky told them. "We're big enough."

"Wait till Mother finds you're missing," Pam said. "She'll be worried!"

Holly explained that she had written a note and left it on their mother's dresser.

"I think I ought to take you back," Kerry said.

"Oh, please don't!" Ricky begged. "Mother and Daddy know we'll be safe with you."

"All right," the acrobat agreed. "If your parents insist that you return, they'll telephone Mrs. Neeley at the gatehouse."

But when they reached there, Kerry's great-aunt had not heard from the Hollisters.

"Either they think it's all right for you to come or they haven't discovered that you're missing," the young man said.

After Mrs. Neeley had praised the youngsters for bringing her and her great-nephew together, Pam gave Ricky her flashlight and the four children trooped behind Kerry toward the front entrance of the old mansion. They entered quietly and talked in whispers.

"Ricky, Holly, you stay here and guard the door," Pete said.

He posted them behind two straight-backed chairs. The rest mounted the staircase, reached the balcony, and stopped once more. There was not a sound.

Now Pete unfolded his plan. He asked Kerry to stand guard at the foot of the stair leading to the third floor. "Pam and I will go to the attic room," he said. "I think it holds the key to this mystery."

"O.K.," Kerry whispered. "If you get into trouble, call me."

Pete and Pam tiptoed up, the boy flicking his light off and on to show the way. Quietly they stepped inside the attic room.

Nothing had been disturbed. The heavy oak chest was exactly where they had seen it before. So was the braided rug.

Pete spoke into his sister's ear. "We'll give this place a good search."

Carefully they felt over the walls. Nothing unusual. Then Pete's fingers followed the edge of the window frame. Finally he reached under the sill. It seemed smooth enough except for one small bump.

Pete flashed his light on it.

"Pam," he whispered, "this looks like a black button."

"Push it!" she urged.

Pete hesitated, not knowing what might happen. "Here goes," he said, taking a deep breath, and pressed with his finger.

There followed a squeaking sound, and the end wall swung inward like a big door.

"It's on a hinge!" Pete said in amazement.

"And there's a room behind it!" Pam added breathlessly.

They stepped forward. The secret place was twice the size of a big closet. Along one side ran a chimney with a great square hole torn away in the bricks. Pete looked into it, shining his light downward and then up.

"Pam, look at this!" She peered into the opening and saw a long stout rope hanging from the top of the chimney down into the basement.

Suddenly she turned to face her brother.

"Now I see the answer! Someone comes through a cellar fireplace and climbs up into this secret room!"

"No wonder we couldn't find the ghost!" Pete said, and accidentally flashed his light upward again. To his astonishment he saw a boxlike contraption tightly attached to the inside of the chimney by a metal strap.

"It's a picture projector, Pam! I'll bet it's responsible for the skeleton in the clouds."

He reached the box and flipped a switch. Instantly

a shaft of light shone up in the chimney. He switched it off quickly.

"Your guess was right, Pete!" his sister said.

So intense was their excitement that they did not hear the squeaking sound start again. By the time they realized what was happening, the swinging wall was nearly closed again.

Pete made a dash for it. Too late. It clicked shut.

"Oh, Pete!" Pam cried, grasping his arm tightly. "We're caught!"

"There must be another button on this side," her brother reasoned, and flashed his light about. It revealed a canvas sack lying in one corner.

The lad bent down and opened it.

"Oh my!" Pam gasped as he shone his light into it.

Before them sparkled a mound of diamond wrist watches, brooches, pearl necklaces, and other jewelry.

"Crickets!" Pete cried. "This is a hide-out for thieves!"

"Probably the same ones Officer Cal is looking for!" said Pam, quivering with excitement.

Pete dug his hands down into the loot and felt something smooth. He pulled out a roll of yellowed papers and spread them open.

"They look like plans of houses," Pam said.

"These must be the ones that were stolen from Mr. Shaffer," Pete replied.

Quickly he found the sketch marked "Miller Mansion." His finger followed the finely drawn line of the chimney to the third floor. There was a tiny room

"It's on a hinge!" Pete said in amazement.

—the very one in which they were trapped. It had a dark "X" crudely marked on it in pencil.

"The thieves discovered this secret room," Pam deduced, "and decided to use it for their hide-out."

"No wonder they were trying to scare Mrs. Neeley and all her customers away," Pete said. "Officer Cal caught one of them. Now if we could only nab the other!"

Just as the brother and sister were about to bang on the walls to alert Kerry Flip, they heard a noise down inside the chimney. Pete shone his light into the black hole. The rope was shaking.

"Oh, Pete!" Pam groaned. "The ghost is returning!"

"This proves he's a live one!" Pete said stoutly, but his knees were trembling.

"If he climbs up here, he'll catch us for sure!" Pam quavered.

CHAPTER 18

TRAPPING A SPOOK

AGAIN Pete threw himself against the wall. It did not budge. Now they could hear the heavy breathing of the man climbing the rope in the chimney.

With shaking fingers, Pam unrolled the plans of the Antique House. Their last hope, she thought, lay in finding a way out of the secret room.

Pete held his flashlight close to the drawings and Pam studied every detail. But no clue. Straining her eyes, she spied a tiny circle marked on the lower left side of the swinging wall.

Swiftly, she dropped to her knees. Pete knelt beside her and shone his light on the spot. Nothing there.

The breathing in the chimney grew louder.

Trembling, Pam felt around the place. There was a faint rectangular outline, as if a block of wood had been inserted.

She banged it with her fist. Pete hit it. Nothing happened. Pam stood up and kicked it hard. Instantly there was a quiet click and a squeaking sound. The wall moved out.

Not waiting to pick up the loot, Pete and Pam

scooted into the attic room and began pushing the door back into place.

Just as it clicked shut they heard the muffled exclamation of the man as he climbed into the secret room.

"Oh, Pete! He'll open it again and catch us!" Pam said. "What'll we do!"

"Here, help me move this," Pete ordered, going to the large chest.

Using every ounce of strength, the two children slid the heavy piece of furniture against the wall. No sooner had they done this when the squeaking started again. The wall moved half an inch but was stopped by the chest.

Pete braced himself hard against it. "Get Kerry!" he commanded. "Call the police! I'll stay here! Hurry."

Pam raced down to the balcony in the dark. "Kerry!" she called. There was no answering voice or light. The girl fairly flew down the next stair. "Ricky!" she called. "Holly!"

A light beamed on near the front door. "We heard a noise. What happened?" Ricky asked, hurrying over to her.

"Where's Kerry?" Pam cried.

"He couldn't find you," Ricky replied.

"So he ran over to Mrs. Neeley's place to call the police," Holly finished quickly.

"There's a man on the third floor," Pam said, "and we have to catch him. Come with me!"

The younger children followed Pam to the door

which led to the cellar. She opened it and tiptoed down the stairs with Ricky and Holly at her heels.

"The chimney's over this way," she remembered as she led the two youngsters through a maze of fruit cellars and storage bins. Ricky flashed his light cautiously to the right and left. Suddenly they saw an open doorway. They stepped through it into a small room with a fireplace. Pam ducked down, then shone her light up the flue.

There was the rope which the "ghost" had climbed!

A gruff voice came hollowly down the chimney. "Who's there? If it's you kids, get away!"

Peering up, Pam saw a pair of hands reach out for the rope. She grabbed the lower end and jiggled it back and forth.

"Hey, stop that! Go away!" came the angry cry. Pam continued to shake the rope until she felt it grow taut.

The man had climbed onto it and was sliding down.

"Help!" Pam yelled. The cry was chorused by Ricky and Holly.

Footsteps sounded on the floor above them. Then came a clattering on the cellar steps.

"What's going on here?" cried a voice which the children recognized immediately.

"Daddy!" Holly called out. "Here we are! Help! Quick!"

In a few moments Mr. Hollister burst into the

small room, followed by Officer Cal and two other policemen. Behind them came Kerry Flip.

"The ghost!" Ricky cried. "He's coming down the chimney."

Suddenly the man's legs appeared in the fireplace. As he touched the ground, Mr. Hollister grabbed his arm, pulled him into the room, and threw him over his shoulder. With a grunt the stocky man landed flat on his back and gems flew out of his pockets.

"Hurray for Daddy!" Ricky shouted.

Officer Cal helped the stunned man to his feet and snapped on handcuffs. "So you're the other ghost who's been haunting this place!" he said.

Before the crestfallen prisoner could reply, the Antique House suddenly was filled with strange sounds of barking dogs, moans, and growling.

"It's still haunted," one of the policemen said.

With Mr. Hollister and the children leading the way, they reached the first floor. "We need more light," their father said, "if we're going to get to the bottom of this." In the beam of Ricky's torch he quickly lit two large antique oil lamps standing on a table. As their glow spread, Pete leaped downstairs.

"Dad!" he cried out. He looked at the handcuffed prisoner and gulped. "So that's the ghost. Boy, is he clever!"

Pete said that while he was holding the wall shut he had noticed several small dials on the wall where the chest had stood.

"I reached over and twisted them," he declared.

"What happened then?" his father asked.

"So you're the other ghost!"

"Wait. I'll go back and do it again," Pete replied eagerly. "You'll see!"

The excited boy raced up the stairs. Presently his voice echoed from the third floor. "I'm turning the dials now!"

All at once weird noises vibrated through the old mansion. Ricky headed for the staircase. "Let's look at the spinning wheel," he cried. Holly and Pam followed.

A moment later Holly called down, "It's turning!"

Just then the grandfather clock in the living room struck thirteen. The girls and Ricky hastened downstairs, followed in a minute by Pete.

"It was all done by electronics," he announced proudly.

"Where did the power come from to run these things?" Kerry asked the prisoner. "There isn't any electricity in the house."

"Walter Kade, you'd better confess!" Officer Cal said, looking sternly at the prisoner.

The man flinched in surprise. "Where did you learn my name?"

"Your pal confessed a few hours ago. He told us you were an electrical expert."

Walter Kade glared at the Hollisters for a moment. Then he hung his head and heaved a big sigh. "Yes, I used batteries and wired this house to frighten people away from it. It was a great idea, but these kids ruined it."

"Why did you play ghost?" Holly piped up.

"I can answer that," Pete interjected. "He's a gem

thief and was using the Antique House as a hide-out for himself and his partner."

The policemen looked on in amazement, hardly able to believe such young children could solve such a baffling mystery.

Pam carried on. "When these men robbed Mr. Shaffer," she said, "they found the plans of old houses around Shoreham. In the sketches of the Antique House they located the secret room, which even Mrs. Neeley didn't know existed."

The prisoner admitted this. He said that he had visited the Antique House, located the attic room, found the button under the window sill, and opened the hidden chamber.

"It was operated by a spring mechanism," the man said. "What a beautiful hide-out!"

"Then you broke an opening into the chimney," Pete reasoned, "and put up the rope for secret entrances and exits."

"You entered through the old tunnel," Mr. Hollister said. "Where does it come into the house?"

"Behind the cellar fireplace," the man replied glumly.

"How did you learn of the tunnel?" Officer Cal queried.

The reply was simple. His buddy, Horace Neman, had worked as a laborer when the culvert was installed. He had marked the pipe where it crossed the old tunnel, in order to cut a hole into the passageway later.

"We had intended to hide in there," the prisoner

said, "but it was too damp and the roof kept caving in."

Realizing that his case was hopeless, Walter Kade talked more freely than ever. Not wishing to be seen around Shoreham, where Neman had a police record, the two men had traveled across the lake from Stony Point in their boat with the yellow motor.

The metal craft was light enough to carry far into the culvert, where it was hidden. When Neman had not shown up at their regular meeting place in Stony Point that night, Kade had been alarmed. He had crossed the lake and climbed the rope to get the jewels and flee.

"So that's why the house was so quiet when we entered," Pam remarked. "You hadn't arrived yet."

"But what made the spinning wheel go and the lamp fall off the table?" Pete asked.

The man explained that he had installed vibrators in several places. Also, he had wired the old clock so that it would strike thirteen times. It was his flashlight, he added, which the children had seen in the attic window.

Upon further questioning, the prisoner admitted sending the warning note and confirmed the deaf boy's guess about the tube of glue.

"Without Charles we might not have solved this case," Pam said. "He was a wonderful help."

"He deserves a medal," Officer Cal said, smiling, "and I'll see to it that he gets one."

Just then there was a shuffling sound at the front

door, and Mrs. Neeley entered, carrying a bright lantern.

"We caught the ghost!" the children said, running over to her.

The woman was amazed to hear what had happened. "You've brought me such happiness," she said, hugging Pam. "You've found me a great-nephew and unhaunted my Antique House."

She looked at each of the children over her glasses and said, "I have a reward for you Hollisters. You may have the grandfather clock which your mother admires so much."

"Yikes!" Ricky cried out. "We can give it to Mommy on her birthday."

"And for the rest of your Detective Club," Mrs. Neeley went on, "we'll have a cookout party by the lake."

"And I'll give them all a special acrobatic performance," Kerry Flip added.

As the police led the prisoner out the front door, Pam called suddenly, "Wait! What about my shoe?"

The prisoner halted and looked back into the room at the old grandfather clock. With a rueful expression he said, "That was the night I really frightened you, wasn't it?"

"You did," Pete confessed, "but you didn't scare us off the case."

The man shook his head slowly. "I took the shoe out of the bushes so you'd think the ghost did it."

"Where did you hide it?" Cal demanded.

"In the back of the grandfather clock!"

Half an hour later the four tired and happy children arrived home with their father. Mrs. Hollister was waiting, eager to hear their story.

As Pete and Pam told her, Ricky said, "Yikes, I'm hungry!"

"Me, too," Holly chirped.

The youngsters skipped into the kitchen. "Let's open a can of something," Ricky suggested.

Holly climbed up to the pantry shelf and selected a large can. The label on it said, "Sweet Potatoes."

"Here," Holly said. "Open it, Ricky. Three guesses what's inside!"

Gerald R. Swanson
Box 335
Silverton, Colorado 81433